DEATH OF A CHARMING MAN

DEATH OF A
CHARMING MAN

M. C. BEATON

THORNDIKE
CHIVERS

This Large Print edition is published by Thorndike Press, Waterville, Maine USA and by BBC Audiobooks Ltd, Bath, England.
Thorndike Press is an imprint of Thomson Gale, a part of The Thomson Corporation.
Thorndike is a trademark and used herein under license.

LIBRARY OF CONGRESS CATALOGING-IN-PUBLICATION DATA

Beaton, M. C.
    Death of a charming man / by M.C. Beaton.
      p. cm. — (Thorndike Press large print mystery)
    "A Hamish Macbeth mystery" — T.p. verso.
    ISBN 0-7862-9046-3 (alk. paper)
    1. MacBeth, Hamish (Fictitious character) — Fiction. 2. Police — Scotland
  — Highlands — Fiction. 3. Highlands (Scotland) — Fiction. I. Title.
PR6053.H4535D38 2006
823'.914—dc22   2006024479

BRITISH LIBRARY CATALOGUING-IN-PUBLICATION DATA AVAILABLE

Published in 2006 in the U.S. by arrangement with Warner Books,
a subsidiary of Hachette Book Group, USA.
Published in 2007 in the U.K. by arrangement with Lowenstein-Yost Inc.

U.S. Hardcover: ISBN 13: 978-0-7862-9046-8; ISBN 10: 0-7862-9046-3
U.K. Hardcover: 978 1 405 63966 8 (Chivers Large Print)
U.K. Softcover: 978 1 405 63967 5 (Camden Large Print)

Printed in the United States of America on permanent paper
10 9 8 7 6 5 4 3 2 1

For Harry Scott Gibbons and
Charles David Bravos Gibbons
with love.

CHAPTER 1

The First Blast of the Trumpet Against the Monstrous Regiment of Women.

John Knox

Hamish Macbeth opened the curtains of his bedroom window, scratched his chest lazily and looked out at the loch. It was a bleached sort of day, the high milky-white cloud with the sun behind it draining colour from the loch, from the surrounding hills, as if the village of Lochdubh were in some art film, changing from colour to black and white. He opened the window and a gust of warm damp air blew in along with a cloud of stinging midges, those Highland mosquitoes. He slammed the window again and turned and looked at his rumpled bed. There had been no crime for months, no villains to engage the attentions of Police Sergeant Macbeth. There was, therefore, no reason why he could not crawl back into that bed and dream another hour away.

And then he heard it . . . faint sounds of scrubbing from the kitchen.

Priscilla!

The sweetness of his unofficial engagement to Priscilla Halburton-Smythe, daughter of a local hotelier and landowner, was fast fading. Cool Priscilla would never deliver herself of such a trite saying as "I am making a man of you, Hamish Macbeth," but that, thought Hamish gloomily, was what she was trying to do. He did not want to be made a man of, he wanted to slouch around the village, gossiping, poaching, and free-loading as he had always done in the tranquil days before his engagement.

There came a grinding of wheels outside, the slamming of doors, and then Priscilla's voice, "Oh, good. Bring it right in here."

Bring what?

He opened the bedroom door and ambled into the kitchen. Where his wood-burning stove had stood, there was a blank space. Two men in uniforms of the Hydro-Electric Board were carrying in a gleaming new electric cooker.

"Whit's this?" demanded Hamish sharply.

Priscilla flashed him a smile. "Oh, Hamish, you lazy thing. It was to be a surprise. I've got rid of that nasty old cooker of yours and bought a new electric one. Surprise!"

Hampered by Highland politeness, Hamish stifled his cry that he wanted his old stove back and mumbled, "Thank you. You shouldnae hae done it."

"Miss Halburton-Smythe!" boomed a voice from the doorway and in lumbered the tweedy figure of Mrs. Wellington, the minister's wife. "I came to see the new cooker," she said. "My, isn't that grand. You're a lucky man, Hamish Macbeth."

Hamish gave a smile which was more like a rictus and backed off. "Aye, chust grand. If you ladies will excuse me, I'll wash and shave."

He went into the newly painted bathroom and looked bleakly at the shower unit over the bath. "Much more hygenic, Hamish. You spend too much time wallowing in the bath," echoed Priscilla's voice in his head.

He washed and shaved at the handbasin, taking a childish pleasure in deciding to have neither shower nor bath. He went back to the bedroom and put on his regulation shirt and trousers and cap. Then he opened the bedroom window and climbed out, feeling a guilty sense of freedom. Towser, his mongrel dog, came bounding around the side of the house to join him. He set off along the waterfront with the dog at his heels. He had forgotten his stick of repellent but was reluctant to go back and fetch it, so he went into Patel's, the general store, and bought a stick. Jessie and Nessie Currie, the spinster sisters, were buying groceries.

"I heard you had the new cooker," said Jessie. "The new cooker." She had an irritating habit of repeating everything.

"You're the lucky man," said Nessie. "We wass just saying the other day, a fine young woman like Miss Halburton-Smythe is mair than you deserve."

"Be the making of you, the making of you," said Jessie.

Hamish smiled weakly and retreated.

He went along and sat on the harbour wall and watched the fishing boats bobbing at anchor. There was something about him, he decided, pushing back his cap and scratching his red hair, which brought out the cleaning beast in people. He had successfully rid himself of Willie Lamont, his police constable, now working at the Italian restaurant, after Willie had nearly driven him mad with his cleaning. The first few heady days of his unofficial engagement to Priscilla had not lasted very long. At first it seemed right that she should start to reorganize the police station, considering she was going to live there. It had to be admitted that the station did need a good clean. But every day? And then she had decided he was not eating properly, and to Hamish's mind nourishing meals meant boring meals, and the more nourishing meals he received from Priscilla's fair hands, the more he thought of going down to Inverness for the day and stuffing himself with junk food. He felt disloyal, but he could not also help feeling rather wistful as he remembered the days when his life had been his own. He remembered reading a letter in an agony column from a "distressed" housewife in which she had complained her husband did not give her enough "space" and he had thought then, cynically, that the woman had little to complain about. Now he knew what she felt. For not only was Priscilla always underfoot, banging pots and pans, but the ladies of the village had taken to calling, and the police station was full of the sound of female voices, all praising Priscilla's improvements. He was sure the police station would be full of them for the rest of the day. A new electric cooker in Lochdubh was the equivalent of a guest appearance by Madonna anywhere else.

He slid down off the wall and headed back

along the waterfront and up out of the village, with Towser loping at his heels. Hamish had decided to go to the Tommel Castle Hotel, now run by Priscilla's father, to see if Mr. Johnston, the manager, would give him a cup of coffee. Priscilla's home seemed to be the one place these days where he was sure he would not run into her.

Mr. Johnston was in his office. He smiled when he saw Hamish and nodded towards the coffee percolator in the corner. "Help yourself, Hamish. It's a long time since you've come mooching around. Where's Priscilla?"

"Herself has chust bought me the new cooker," said Hamish over his shoulder as he poured a mug of coffee.

Mr. Johnston knew of old that Hamish's accent became more sibilant when the police sergeant was upset.

"Oh, aye," said the hotel manager, eyeing the rigidity of Hamish's thin back. "Well, that's marriage for ye. Nothing like the ladies for getting life sorted out."

"I'm a lucky man," said Hamish repressively. He never discussed Priscilla with anyone. He often wondered if there was anyone he could discuss her with, even if he had wanted to. Everyone, particularly his own mother, kept telling him how lucky he was.

"You might not be seeing so much of her in the next week or two," said Mr. Johnston.

"And why is that?" Hamish sat down on the opposite side of the desk and sipped his coffee.

"Hotel's going to be full up. The maids keep going off work with one excuse or the other. So you won't be seeing much of her, like I said. You need a crime to keep you going."

"I don't get bored," said Hamish mildly. "I am not looking for the crime to keep me amused."

The hotel manager looked at the tall gangling policeman with affection. "I often wonder why you ever bothered to join the police force, Hamish. Why not jist be a Highland layabout, draw the dole, poach a bit?"

"Oh, the police suits me chust fine. Also, if I had the big crime here again, they might send me an assistant and I could not be doing with being scrubbed out o' house and home."

"So what are you doing here when you ought to be wi' your sweetie? A rare hand with the scrubbing brush is our Priscilla, talking about being scrubbed out."

Hamish looked at him blankly and Mr. Johnston suddenly felt he had been impertinent. "Well, I've a wee bit o' gossip for you," he said hurriedly. "Drim is on your beat, isn't it?"

"Aye, but nothing's ever happened there and never will. It must be the dullest place in the British Isles."

"Oh, but something has happened. Beauty's come to Drim and it ain't a lassie but a fellow. Folks say he's like a film star."

"What brings him to a place like Drim?"

"God knows. Jist strolled into the village one day, bought a wee bit of a croft house and started doing it up. Posh chap. English."

"Oh, one o' them."

"Aye, he'll play at being a villager for a bit and talk about the simple life and then one winter up here will send him packing."

"The winters aren't so bad."

"I amnae talking about the weather, Hamish. I'm talking about that shut-down feeling that happens up here in the winter where you sit and think the rest of the world has gone off somewhere to have a party, leaving you alone in a black wilderness."

"I don't feel like that."

"No? Well, I suppose it's because I'm from the city," said Mr. Johnston, who came from Glasgow.

14

"I might take a look over at Drim and pay a visit to this fellow," said Hamish. "Any chance of borrowing one of the hotel cars?"

"What's happened to the police Land Rover?"

Hamish shifted awkwardly. "It's down at the police station. I walked here. Chust wanted to save myself the walk back."

"Well, if you're not going to have it away too long," said Mr. Johnston, stopping himself in time from pointing out that when Hamish returned the car, he would still have to walk back to Lochdubh. He opened the desk drawer and fished out a set of car keys. "Take the Volvo. But don't keep it out all day. The new guests will be arriving. I'll just give Priscilla a ring and tell her she'd better be here to welcome them."

Hamish took the keys and strolled off. As he drove out on the road to Drim, he felt as if he were on holiday, as if he were driving away from the monstrous regiment of women, the rule of women as John Knox had meant, the one particular woman in his life who was hell-bent on making a success-ful man of him. Priscilla had determinedly set out to make friends with the wife of Chief Superintendent Peter Daviot. Hamish knew Priscilla wanted him to be promoted higher. But promotion meant living in

15

Strathbane, promotion meant exams, promotion meant becoming a detective and never being allowed back to Lochdubh again. He shoved his worried thoughts firmly to the back of his mind.

The wind was rising and tearing the milky clouds into ragged wisps. The sun shone fitfully down, the heather blazed purple along the flanks of the mountains, and as he gained the crest of a hill he looked down across a breath-taking expanse of mountain and moorland, with the tarns of Sutherland gleaming sapphire-blue among the heather where the clumsy grouse stumbled, flapped, and rose before the swift feet of a herd of deer.

He concentrated his mind on wondering what had brought this Adonis to a place like Drim.

Drim was a peculiar place at the end of a thin sea loch on a flat piece of land surrounded by towering black mountains. The loch itself was black, a corridor of a loch between the high walls of the mountains where little grew among the scree and black rock but stunted bushes. The only access to Drim, unless one was foolhardy enough to brave a trip by sea, was by a narrow one-track road over the hills from the east. The village was a huddle of houses with a church, a community hall, a general store, but no police station. The village was policed from Lochdubh by Hamish Macbeth, although the villagers hardly ever saw him. There had never been any crime in Drim, not even drunkenness, for there was no pub, and no alcohol for sale.

He parked the car and went into the general store run by a giant of a man called Jock Kennedy. "Hamish," said Jock, "have not seen you in ages. What iss bringing you to us?"

"Just curiosity," said Hamish. "I hear you've got an incomer."

"Oh, aye. Peter Hynd. Nice young man. Bought that old croft house o' Geordie Black's up above the village. Putting in his own drains. Old Geordie just used a hut out the back for a toilet and there wasnae a bathroom, old Geordie not believing in washing all ower except for funerals and weddings."

"Geordie's dead then?"

"Aye, died six month ago, and his daughter sold the house. She was as surprised as anyone, I am telling you, when this young fellow offered her the money for it. She thocht it would be lying there until it fell to bits."

"I might just go and hae a wee word with

him," said Hamish. He bought a bottle of fizzy lemonade and two sausage rolls and ate and drank, sitting outside on a bench in front of the shop. Priscilla, he thought with a stab of guilt, would no doubt have prepared a nourishing lunch for him, brown rice and something or other. He should have phoned her.

The loch was only a few yards away, its black waters sucking at the oily stones on the beach. Everything was very quiet and still. The mountains shut out the wind and shut out most of the light. A grim, sad place. What on earth was a beautiful young Englishman doing here?

The village consisted of several cottages grouped about the store. It was a Highland village that time had forgotten. The only new building was the ugly square community hall with its tin roof, its walls painted acid-sulphurous yellow. Behind the hall was the church, a small stone building with a Celtic cross at one end of the roof and an iron bell at the other. Hamish realized with surprise that although he knew Jock Kennedy, he hardly knew anyone else in this odd village to speak to. He rose and stretched and gave the last of one of his sausage rolls to Towser and then set out for Peter Hynd's cottage.

He heard the sounds of pick on rock as he approached. It was an ugly little grey cottage with a corrugated-iron roof. A new fence had been put around a weedy garden where no flowers grew. He walked round the cottage towards the sound of the pick and there, down a trench, working industriously, stripped to the waist, was the most beautiful man Hamish had ever seen. He stopped his work, put down the pick, scrambled nimbly out of the trench and stood looking at Hamish, his hands on his hips.

Peter Hynd was about five feet ten inches in height. His face and body were lightly tanned a golden brown. His figure was slim and well-muscled. He had golden hair which curled on his head like a cap. He had high cheek-bones and golden-brown eyes framed with thick lashes. His mouth was firm and well-shaped and his neck was the kind of neck that classical sculptors dream about.

"Hullo," he said. "Is this visit official?"

"No," said Hamish, "Just a friendly call."

Peter smiled suddenly and Hamish blinked as though before a sudden burst of sunlight. That smile illuminated the young man's face with a radiance. "You'd better come indoors," said Peter, "and have something. Tea or coffee?"

"Coffee would be chust fine," said Hamish, feeling suddenly shy.

Peter took a checked shirt off a nail on the fence and put it on. His accent was light, pleasant, upper-class but totally without drawl or affectation.

Hamish followed him into the house, ducking his head as he did so, for the doorway was low. The cottage was in the usual old-fashioned croft-house pattern, living-room with a fire for cooking on to one side and parlour to the other. Peter had transformed the living-room into a sort of temporary kitchen, with a counter along one side with shelves containing dishes, and pots and pans above it. In the centre of the room was a scrubbed kitchen table surrounded by high-backed chairs. Peter put a kettle on a camping stove at the edge of the table. "I used that old kettle on the chain over the fire when I first arrived," he said with a grin, "but it took ages to boil. The peat around here doesn't give out much heat. Milk and sugar?"

"Just black," said Hamish, beginning to feel more at ease.

"I'm building a kitchen at the back," said Peter, taking down two mugs.

"What are you doing in the garden?"

asked Hamish.

"Digging drains and a cesspool. I plan to have a flushing toilet and a bathroom. You've no idea what it's like when you want a pee in the middle of the night and have to go out to that hut in the garden."

"You might find it difficult to get help," said Hamish. "The locals can be a bit stand-offish."

Peter looked surprised. "On the contrary, I've had more offers of help than I can cope with. People are very kind. I didn't know we had a policeman."

"You don't. I'm over at Lochdubh. This is part of my beat."

"Much crime?"

"Verra quiet, I'm glad to say."

"Macbeth, Macbeth. That rings a bell. Oh, I know. You've been involved in some murder cases up here."

"Yes, but I am hoping neffer to be involved in another. Thank you for the coffee."

Peter sat down opposite Hamish and stretched like a cat. A good thing there were no young women in Drim, thought Hamish, with this heart-breaker around.

"Do you plan to stay here?" he asked curiously.

"Yes, why not?"

"But you're a young man. There's nothing

for you here."

"On the contrary, I think I've found what I'm looking for."

"That being?"

There was a slight hesitation. Hamish shivered suddenly. "Tranquillity," said Peter vaguely. "Building things, working with my hands."

Hamish finished his coffee and got up to leave.

"Come again," said Peter and again there was that blinding smile.

Hamish smiled back. "Aye, I will that, and maybe next time I'll give you a hand."

Hamish walked away from the cottage still smiling, but as he reached the car parked in the village his smile faded. He gave himself a little shake. There was no doubt that Peter Hynd possessed great charm. But out of his orbit, Hamish found himself almost disliking the man, almost afraid of him, and wondered why. With a little sigh he opened the passenger door for Towser to leap in, before getting into the driver's seat.

His spirits lifted when he drove up the hill out of Drim and into the sunshine. There was no need to go back to Drim for some time, no need at all.

He parked the hotel car in the forecourt of Tommel Castle and then walked into the hotel and handed the keys to Mr. Johnston.

"Priscilla's back," said the hotel manager. "Will I let her know you're here?"

"No, no," said Hamish. "I've got my chores to do. I'll phone her later."

He hurried off. Five minutes later Priscilla walked into the hotel office. "Someone told me they had seen Hamish and Towser walking off," she said.

"Aye, he said he couldnae wait. He had chores to do."

"I wonder what those could be," said Priscilla cynically. "All he's got to do is put the dinner I left him in his new oven. Did he tell you about the electric cooker?"

"Yes, he did mention it. Did you ask him if he wanted a new cooker?"

"No, why? There was no reason to. That old stove was a disgrace."

"I think he liked it," said Mr. Johnston cautiously. "Cosy in the winter."

"He's got central heating now."

"Aye, but there's nothing like a real fire. You won't change Hamish, Priscilla."

"I am not trying to change him," snapped Priscilla. "You forget, I'm going to have to live in that police station myself."

"Oh, well, suit yourself."

"In fact, I might just run down there. I left the instruction booklet for the new cooker on the table, but you know Hamish."

"Aye, he's a grown man and not a bairn."

Priscilla fidgeted nervously with a pencil on the desk. "Nonetheless, I'll just go and see how he's doing."

Mr. Johnston shook his head sadly after she had left. It was as if the usually cool and calm Priscilla had taken up a cause and that cause was the advancement of Hamish Macbeth.

Priscilla pulled up outside the police station. Dr. Brodie was walking past and raised his cap.

The doctor was one of the few people in the village opposed to the forthcoming marriage of Hamish Macbeth and Priscilla Halburton-Smythe. He saw over Priscilla's shoulder as she got out of her car the approaching figure of Hamish at the far end of the waterfront. Priscilla must have passed him on the road without seeing him.

"If you're looking for Hamish," said Dr. Brodie, "he's gone off to see Angus Macdonald."

"That old fraud!"

"He's been feeling poorly."

Priscilla opened her car door again. "I may as well rescue him before Angus pretends to tell his future."

She drove off, swinging the car round.

That was childish of me, thought the doctor. I was only trying to give Hamish a break, but she's bound to see him.

But as he looked along the waterfront, there was no sign of Hamish. Priscilla's car sped out of view. Then Hamish reappeared. Dr. Brodie grinned. Hamish must have dived for cover. Priscilla should be marrying one of her own kind, he thought, old-fashioned snobbery mixing with common sense.

Angus Macdonald had gained a certain fame as a seer. Priscilla thought he was a shrewd old man who listened to all the village gossip and made his predictions accordingly.

When she drove up it was to see the old man working in his garden. He waved to her and beckoned.

She went forward reluctantly. The Land Rover had been outside the police station. Hamish surely would not have bothered walking.

"Dr. Brodie said you were not feeling well," said Priscilla. "Where's Hamish?"

"Why should he say that? I havenae seen Hamish."

"I'd better be getting back."

"Och, stay a minute and give an auld man

25

the pleasure of your company."

Priscilla followed the seer into his cottage, noticing with irritation that he was putting the kettle on the peat fire to boil. With the money he conned out of people, she thought, he could well afford to buy something modern.

But she politely asked after his health and learned to her increasing irritation that it was "neffer better."

Angus settled down finally over the teapot and asked her a lot of searching questions about people in the village. "I thought you were a seer," said Priscilla finally and impatiently. "You are supposed to know all this by just sitting on your backside and dreaming."

"I see things all right." Angus Macdonald was a tall, thin man in his sixties. He had a thick head of white hair and a craggy face with an enormous beak of a nose. He smiled at Priscilla and said, "I see your future." His voice had taken on an odd crooning note. Priscilla, despite herself, felt hypnotized. "You will not marry Macbeth. A beautiful man will come between you."

Priscilla burst out laughing. "Oh, Angus, *honestly.* There is nothing homosexual about Hamish."

"I wisnae saying that. I see a beautiful

young man and he's going to come between you two."

Priscilla picked up her handbag. "I've no intention of being unfaithful to Hamish either. Beautiful young man, indeed."

She drove down to the police station, but as she was raising her hand to knock at the kitchen door, she heard the sound of masculine laughter coming from inside. She walked around the back of the house and glanced in the kitchen window. Hamish and Dr. Brodie were sitting at the kitchen table, an open whisky bottle in front of them. Hamish appeared more relaxed and amused than Priscilla had seen him look for some time.

She walked away and got back in the car. Surely Dr. Brodie could not have been deliberately lying to her about Angus. But she felt reluctant to go in there and face him with it. Besides, the new guests would be arriving about now at the hotel. She would feel more like her old self when she got down to work. She always felt better these days when she was working.

When she arrived at the hotel, Mr. Johnston popped his head outside the office door and said, "Thon Mrs. Daviot's on the line for you."

Priscilla brightened. The Chief Superin-

tendent's wife. "Hallo, Mrs. Daviot," she
said.

"Now didn't I tell you to call me Susan?"
said Mrs. Daviot coyly. "Ai have been thinking, Priscilla, dear, that there are some vairy
nice houses around Strathbane. If Hamish
got a promotion, you'd need to live here. It
wouldn't do any hairm to look at just a few
of them."

"I suppose not," said Priscilla cautiously.
"But Hamish might not like it. He's set on
staying in Lochdubh."

"All that young man needs is a push," said
Mrs. Daviot. "Once you get him out of
Lochdubh, he'll forget the place existed."

CHAPTER 2

What ills from beauty spring
                              Samuel Johnson

Hamish was surprised to find the next day passed without his seeing Priscilla. The short absence rapidly made the heart grow fonder, and he forgot her cleaning and remembered her kisses. The cooker gleamed in the corner of his dark kitchen in all its pristine glory and he felt he had been sparing in his thanks, to say the least.

By late evening, he was just making up his mind to phone her when Priscilla herself arrived in a cloud of French perfume.

"My, you look grand," said Hamish, standing back to admire a short black silk skirt, black stockings, and a glittering evening top.

"We had a reception for the guests, a computer company with money to burn. Nothing but the best. Gosh, I am tired."

He noticed for the first time how thin she had become, and the shadows under her eyes.

"You'll need to learn to relax," he said.

Priscilla sighed. "I don't think I know how to."

"I'll show you," he said huskily. He wrapped his long arms about her and held her close, and then he kissed her with all his heart and soul. For one dizzying moment she responded, and then he felt her go rigid in his arms. He drew back a little and looked down at her. She was staring over his shoulder at a corner of the kitchen ceiling.

"What's the matter?" asked Hamish, twisting his head to follow her gaze.

"There's a great big cobweb up there. How could I have missed it?"

"Priscilla, forget the bloody cobweb, forget the cleaning, come to bed." His fingers began to unbutton the back of her top.

She twisted away from him. "Not now, Hamish, there'll be time enough for that when we are married."

Priscilla blushed the minute the awful words were out of her mouth, those trite words, the cry of the suburban prude. "See you tomorrow, Hamish." She gave him a quick peck on the cheek and almost ran out of the door.

As she drove back to Tommel Castle, the seer's words rang in her head. But if she gave in to Hamish now, she would never have the strength to realize her ambitions for him, and all Hamish Macbeth needed was a *push.*

When she reached the hotel, she was met in the reception by Mr. Johnston. "You'll need to take over the bar, Priscilla, for the last hour. Roger's fallen down." Roger was the barman.

"Drunk?" asked Priscilla.

"Again."

"Been pinching the drinks?"

"No," said Mr. Johnston. "I'll say that much for him. But the customers will say, 'Have one yourself, Roger,' and he does, and the maids can't mix the fancy drinks."

"Where's my father?"

"Gone tae his bed."

"I'll do it."

"You'd better button up the back of that blouse," remarked Mr. Johnston. "It's nearly falling off you."

Priscilla blushed again. "Here, I'll do it." The manager buttoned her up, smiling his approval of what he took to be a hopeful sign that Hamish was getting down to business at last.

The bar, to Priscilla's relief, was not very full. She relieved the maid, Jessie, who was plaintively asking a customer how to make a Manhattan. The bar closed at eleven. Priscilla glanced at the clock. Not too long to go. Then, as one by one the guests left to go to their rooms or through to watch television, she noticed one of the most beautiful young men she had ever seen sitting at a table in the corner. He was reading a magazine and had a half-finished pint of beer in front of him. His golden hair gleamed softly in the overhead lights and his long eyelashes cast shadows on his tanned cheeks. He looked up and saw her watching him and gave her a slow, intimate smile, and Priscilla found herself smiling back. Another customer came up and she forgot about the beautiful young man for the moment, but just before closing time he came up to the bar and said, "Have I time for another?"

"Just," said Priscilla. "Another pint?"

"I'll have a whisky to see me on my way."

"Make sure you're not over the limit," said Priscilla, holding a glass under the optic. "The police can be quite strict."

"I shouldn't think Hamish Macbeth would be too strict about anything" came his voice from behind her.

She felt a sudden superstitious stab of fear. Was this Angus's beautiful young man? But she turned around and, putting the glass on the bar, said, "So you know our local copper."

"He paid a call on me. I live in Drim."

"Do you have relatives there?"

He paid for his drink. "No, I just wandered in one day and stayed. What about you?"

"My parents run this hotel."

"Poor you. Hard work, I should think. Ever get a night off?"

"From time to time, when we're not too busy."

"You must come over to Drim and see my place," he said, leaning easily on the bar. He held out his hand. "Peter Hynd."

"Priscilla Halburton-Smythe." Priscilla took his hand and then gave him a startled look as something like an electric charge went from his hand up her arm. "I'm not free even on my nights off," she said. "I am engaged to be married, and that takes up my time."

"Who's the lucky man?"

"Hamish Macbeth."

He stood back a little and surveyed the cool and sophisticated Priscilla from the top of her smooth blonde head to the expensive

French evening top, which was as much as he could see of her behind the bar. "Well, well, well," he said. "You amaze me."

Priscilla gave herself a mental shake. Peter Hynd was talking to her as if he had known her for a long time, not so much by his words as by his manner, which seemed to be creating a heady atmosphere of intimacy. To her relief another customer came up and Peter took his whisky and retreated to his corner.

He stayed in the bar until she closed it down and pulled the grille over it. He looked about to speak to her again but she quickly left the bar and went to see Mr. Johnston. She experienced the same feeling as Hamish had had — that once she was out of Peter's magic orbit, she found she neither liked him nor trusted him. "I must tell Hamish," she thought, but then forgot all about the meeting until some time later.

Over in Drim the next day, Miss Alice Mac-Queen was up early to prepare for business, and business had never been so good. She was the village hairdresser and worked from the front parlour of her cottage. Before the arrival of Peter Hynd, she had not been very busy, the women of Drim getting their hair permed about once a year, usually before

Christmas. But now her services were in demand, and the number of greyheads who wanted to be dyed blonde or black was mounting.

Mrs. Edie Aubrey was also preparing for a busy day. For the past six months, she had been trying to run an exercise class in the community hall but without much success. Now her classes were suddenly full of sweating village women determined to reduce their massive bums and bosoms.

In the general store, Jock Kennedy unpacked a new consignment of cosmetics and put them on display. He had found the women were travelling to Strathbane to pay a fortune for the latest in anti-wrinkle creams and decided it was time he made some money out of the craze for youth that the incomer had roused in so many middle-aged bosoms. As his own wife seemed unaffected, he was one of the few in the village who was not troubled by Peter Hynd. Drim did not have any young women, apart from teenagers at school. The school-leaving daughters took off for the cities to find work.

Jimmy Macleod, a crofter, came in from the fields for his dinner, which, as in most of the homes in Drim, was still served in the middle of the day.

His meal consisted of soup, mince and

potatoes, and strong tea. He ate while reading a newspaper, folded open at the sports section and propped against the milk jug. He had just finished reading when he realized that something was different. In the first place, his wife should have been sitting opposite him instead of fiddling over at the kitchen sink.

"Arenae you eating?" He looked up and his mouth fell open. "Whit haff you been doin't tae your hair?"

For his wife Nancy's normally grey locks were now jet-black and cut in that old-fashioned chrysanthemum style of the fifties, which was the best that Alice Mac-Queen could achieve. Not only that, but Nancy's normally high colour was hidden under a mask of foundation cream and powder and her lips were painted scarlet.

She patted her hair with a nervous hand. "Got tired o' looking old," she said. She turned back to the sink and began to clatter the dishes with unnecessary energy.

"You look daft," he said with scorn. "And that muck on your face makes you look like a hooker."

"And what would you know aboot hookers, wee man?"

"Mair o' your lip and I'll take my belt tae ye."

She turned round slowly and lifted up the bread knife. "Chust you try," she said softly.

"Hey, I'm oot o' here till ye come tae your senses," he said. He was a small, wiry man with rounded shoulders and a crablike walk. He scuttled out the door. For the first time he regretted the fact that Drim was a "dry" village. He felt he could do with a large whisky. He headed out to the fields. His neighbour, Andrew King, hailed him.

"Looking a bit grim, Jimmy."

"Women," growled Jimmy, walking up to him. "My Nancy's got her face painted like a tart and she's dyed her hair black. Aye, and she threatened me wi' the bread knife. Whit's the world coming tae?"

"Ye've got naethin' tae worry about," said Andrew, an older crofter whose nutcracker face was seamed and wrinkled. "I 'member when my Jeannie went daft. You know whit it was?"

"No, that I don't."

"It's the Men's Paws."

"The whit?"

"The Men's Paws. The change. Drives the women fair daft, that it does. I talked to the doctor about Jeannie and he said, 'Jist ignore it and it'll go away,' and so it did." Andrew fished in the capacious pocket of his coat and produced a half bottle of

37

whisky. "Like a pull?"

"Man, I would that. But don't let the minister see us!"

Drim's minister, Mr. Callum Duncan, was putting the finishing touches to his sermon. He gave a sigh of satisfaction. He would now have free time to write to his son in Edinburgh and his daughter in London.

"I'm just going to write to Agnes and Diarmuid," he said to his wife, who was sitting sewing by the window. "Do you want to add a note?"

"I wrote to them both yesterday," said his wife, Annie.

"Well, you'd better tell me what you told them so I don't repeat the gossip." The minister rose and stretched. He was a slight man with thinning grey hair, grey eyes, and a trap of a mouth. Annie had begun recently to hate that mouth, which always seemed to be clamped shut in disapproval.

A shaft of sunlight shone in the window and lit up Annie's hair. The minister stared at his wife. "What have you been doing to your hair?"

"I put a red rinse on it," she said calmly. "Jock has some new stuff. It washes out."

"What's up with brown hair?" he demanded crossly. He had always considered his wife's thick brown hair her one beauty.

"I got tired of it," she said with a little sigh. "Don't make a fuss about trivia, Callum. It wearies me." And she went on sewing.

Harry Baxter drove his battered old truck down the winding road to Drim. He was a fisherman. There had been a bad-weather forecast and so the fishing boat at Lochdubh that he worked on had decided not to put out to sea. He was chewing peppermints because he had spent part of the morning in the Lochdubh bar, and like most of the men in Drim he liked to maintain the fiction that he never touched liquor. Just outside the village he saw a shapely woman with bright-blonde hair piled up on her head tottering along on very high heels. Her ample hips swayed as she walked. He grinned and rolled down the window and pursed up his lips to give a wolf whistle. Then he realized there was an awful familiarity about that figure and drew his truck alongside.

"Hullo, Harry," said his wife, Betty.

"Oh, my God," he said slowly in horror. "You look a right mess."

"It was time I did something tae masel'," she said, heaving her plump shoulders in a shrug. She was carrying a pink holdall.

"We'd better go home and talk about this," he said. "Hop in."

"Can't," she said laconically. "I'm off to Edie's exercise class." And she turned on those ridiculous heels and swayed off.

There was a fine drizzle falling by early evening. Stripped to the waist and with raindrops running down his golden chest, Peter Hynd worked diligently, as if oblivious to the row of village women standing silently watching him. Rain dripped down on bodies sore from unaccustomed exercise and on newly dyed hair. Feet ached in thin high-heeled shoes. And beyond the women the men of the village gathered — small sour men, wrinkled crablike men, men who watched and suddenly knew the reason for all the beautifying.

"Men's Paws," sneered Jimmy Macleod, spitting on the ground.

Several days later, Hamish was strolling along the waterfront with his dog at his heels and his cap pushed on the back of his head. A gusty warm wind was blowing in from the Gulf Stream and banishing the midges for one day at least. Everything danced in the wind: the fishing boats at anchor, the roses and sweet peas in the gardens, and the washing on the lines. Busy little waves slapped at the shore, as if applauding one indolent policeman's progess.

And then a car drew up beside him. Hamish smiled down and then his face took on a guarded, cautious look. For the driver was Susan Daviot, wife of his Chief Superintendent. She was a sturdy woman who always looked as if she were on her way to a garden party or a wedding, for she always wore a hat, one of those hats that had gone out of fashion at the end of the fifties but were still sold in some Scottish backwaters. This day's number was of maroon felt with a feather stuck through the front of it. She had a high colour which showed under the floury-white powder with which she dusted her face. Her mouth was small and pursed. "Ai'll be coming beck with Priscilla to pick you up," said Mrs. Daviot.

"I am on duty," said Hamish stiffly.

"Don't be silly. I told Peter I was taking you off for the day. There is this dehrling house just outside Strathbane I want you and Priscilla to see."

Hamish opened his mouth to protest that he had no intention of moving to Strathbane or anywhere near it, but realized that would bring a lecture about his lack of

41

ambition down on his head, so he said, "But didn't you hear? Trouble over at Drim."

"What sort of trouble?"

Hamish looked suitably mysterious. "I would rather not be saying at the moment."

Mrs. Daviot grunted and drove off. Not for the first time did she think that Priscilla was not making a most suitable marriage, but on the other hand, had her husband not been Hamish Macbeth's boss, then she would never have had the opportunity to go house-hunting with such an exalted personage as Priscilla.

"Now, look what I've done," said Hamish to Towser. "Why didn't I stand up for myself? Och, well, we'll chust run over to Drim. A grand day for it."

He walked back to the police station, lifted Towser, who was as lazy as his master and would not jump, into the back of the Land Rover, and drove off. As he plunged down the heathery track which led into Drim, he felt he was leaving all air and sunlight behind. The village lay dark and silent, staring at its reflection in the loch.

He parked outside Jock Kennedy's store. It was the school holidays, yet no children played, although in these modern times that was not so unusual. Probably they were all indoors playing video games.

42

The shop had a CLOSED sign hanging on the door. Half day. He thought that they were all truly spoiled over in Lochdubh since Patel had taken over the store there. Patel was open from eight in the morning until ten at night, seven days a week.

With Towser loping behind him, he made his way up to the manse. The minister would surely be good for a cup of tea. The manse was a square Victorian building built beside the loch, with a depressing garden of weedy grass and rhododendrons. It had been built in the days when ministers had large families, and Hamish guessed was probably full of unused rooms. He went round to the kitchen door and knocked.

After some minutes the minister's wife, Annie Duncan, answered the door. She was a slight woman with good, well-spaced features and long brown hair highlighted with red. "Has anything happened?" she asked, staring anxiously at Hamish's uniform.

"No, I was on my beat and I thought I would pay my respects," said Hamish.

She hesitated. "Callum, my husband, is out on his rounds at the moment. Perhaps . . . perhaps you would like a cup of coffee?"

"That would be grand."

She looked for a moment as if she wished he had refused and then turned away, leaving him to follow. He found himself in a large stone-flagged kitchen. The room was dark and felt cold, even on this summer's day. It seemed to exude an aura of Victorian kitchen slavery. A huge dresser dominated one wall, full of blue-and-white plates and those giant tureens and serving dishes of the last century. She spooned coffee out of a jar into a jug, took an already boiling kettle off the Aga cooker, and filled the jug. "I'll leave this to settle for a moment," said Annie. "Sit down, Mr. . . .?"

"Macbeth."

"From Lochdubh?"

"The same."

"So what brings you here?"

"As I said, Drim is on my beat. It's not as if anything has happened."

"Nothing ever happens in Drim."

"Except for your newcomer, Peter Hynd. I've met him."

For one moment her face blazed with an inner radiance in the dark kitchen and then her habitual shuttered look closed down on it. "Yes, he is a charming boy," she said in a neutral voice. She poured a mug of coffee and handed it to him.

"An odd sort of place for a man like that

to settle," remarked Hamish. "I mean, what is there for him here?"

"What is there for any of us?"

"I mean," pursued Hamish, "the north of Scotland is home to us, but it's a cut-off sort of place, and there's no place on the mainland more cut off than Drim. At least in Lochdubh, we get the tourists."

She clasped her thin fingers around the cup as if for warmth and held the cup to her chest. "I am not from here," she said. "I am from London."

"And how long have you been in Drim?"

"For twenty-five years," she said. She made it sound like a prison sentence. "I met Callum when I was on holiday in Edinburgh. We got married. At first it seemed so romantic. I read all those Jacobite novels, Bonnie Prince Charlie and all that; I read up on the clan histories. The children came, and that took up time. Now they are grown up and gone and there is just Callum and me . . . and Drim."

Hamish shifted uneasily, wanting to escape. He had once visited someone in prison in Inverness. He experienced again the same suffocating feeling and desire to escape as he had had then.

He drained his cup. "Aye, well, that was the grand cup of coffee, Mrs. Duncan. I'll be on my way."

She gave him a controlled little smile. "Call in any time you are passing," she said.

Hamish made his way out and took in great lungfuls of air. Towser, who had been left in the garden, wagged his tail lazily. "Since we're here," said Hamish to the dog, "we may as well look in on Jimmy Macleod." He did not know the crofter very well but he was strangely reluctant to call on Peter Hynd again and reluctant to return so soon to Lochdubh, where he still might be scooped up by Mrs. Daviot and Priscilla to go house-hunting.

He wandered in the direction of the croft, which lay just outside the village. Damp sheep cropped steadily at the wet grass. The ground in Drim always seemed to be wet underfoot. He could see Jimmy two fields away, hammering in a fencepost. He made his way across to him.

"What's up?" cried Jimmy in alarm as he approached. The residents of Lochdubh automatically supposed — and rightly — when Hamish arrived on their doorsteps that he was on a mooching raid, but to the residents of Drim the sight of a policeman still meant bad news.

"Nothing," said Hamish, walking up to him. "I should come to Drim mair often, then you'd all get used to me. I feel like the angel of death."

Jimmy gave the fence-post another vicious slam with the sledge-hammer. "Fancy a bit o' dinner? Nancy aye cooks enough fur a regiment."

"That's verra kind of you," said Hamish, falling into step beside the crofter. "Anything happening in Drim?"

"Naethin'," said Jimmy curtly.

They walked on in silence until they reached the low croft house. Hamish followed him into the kitchen. "I've brought a visitor, Nancy," said Jimmy. "Manage another dinner."

"Aye," she said curtly and threw another mackerel on the frying pan. "If you don't mind," said Hamish to her back, "I would like a bowl of water for my dog."

She reached out and seized a bowl from the drying rack and slammed it down in front of him. "Help yoursel'."

Hamish filled the bowl with water and put it down in front of Towser. The tension in the kitchen between the married couple seemed to crackle in the air.

"Sit yourself down," ordered Jimmy, and so Hamish sat down, wishing he had not accepted the crofter's invitation. Jimmy stared at the centre of the table. The mackerel hissed in the pan. As if sensing the atmosphere, Towser gave a heavy sigh and lay down with his head on his paws.

Nancy slammed plates of food down in front of Hamish and Jimmy and said, "I'm off."

"You'll stay right where you are, wumman," growled Jimmy.

She tossed her dyed black hair and went out of the room.

Jimmy picked at his mackerel and then threw down his knife and fork and went out.

Hamish could hear him mounting the stairs to where he supposed the bedrooms lay, under the roof. He tried not to listen but they were shouting at each other.

"Ye're makin' a fool o' yoursel' wi' a fellow half your age, you silly auld biddy."

"Get stuffed," came Nancy's reply. "You dinnae own me."

"I've had enough. Hear this, Nancy Macleod; if you don't come tae yir senses, I'll murder that English bastard."

"Ach, get oot o' my way, ye wee ferret, or I'll murder you."

There came the sound of a blow followed by a cry, and then the deafening crack of a slap and Nancy's voice shouting shrilly, "Take that, bastard, and neffer lay the hand on me again."

Hamish half-rose in his seat. He hated "domestics," as marital fights were called in the police. But he heard Jimmy clattering down the stairs and sat down again quickly.

Jimmy came in, one cheek bright-red. He sat down and picked up his knife and fork, his calloused hands trembling. Then he threw them down and began to cry.

"There, now," said Hamish, standing up and going round to put a comforting hand on his shoulder. "There, now."

"I'll kill that English bastard, that I will," sobbed Jimmy. "He's bringing grief tae us all. The women have all gone fair daft."

"Is he doing anything to encourage the women?" asked Hamish.

"Jist smiles and smiles, kisses them like a Frenchie, smarms all ower them."

"I'll maybe be haein' a wee word with him," said Hamish. He saw a whisky bottle on the kitchen counter and went over and poured a glassful. "Get that down ye."

"Neffer had the drink in the hoose except at Hogmanay," said Jimmy, "until this happened."

The kitchen door opened and Nancy stood there. Her figure had changed dramatically, due, thought Hamish, to some sort of rigid corseting. Her face was highly made up. Her eyes reflected a mixture of wariness and defiance.

"I'm off," she said and slammed out.

Jimmy drank whisky and ate steadily. Finally he pushed his plate away and rolled and lit a cigarette. Hamish sniffed the air. It was some time since he himself had had a cigarette, but he suddenly had a craving for one.

"Where's she gone?" he asked.

"One o' three places. She goes tae Alice MacQueen's tae get her hair done, or she goes tae that silly biddy Edie Aubrey's exercise class, or she goes wi' the others tae lean over the fence at Hynd's and gawp at him like a lot o' coos."

"I think I'll chust go over tae Peter Hynd's and talk to him," said Hamish. "Neffer mind, Jimmy. You know these incomers. They neffer stay long."

Jimmy said nothing.

Hamish roused the now sleeping Towser and went off. He was beginning to feel very uneasy. As he approached the community hall, he could hear the sound of music. He stood on tiptoe and looked in one of the windows.

To the sound of the music from *Saturday Night Fever,* the women of Drim gyrated and sweated. Great bosoms bobbed and heaved, and massive backsides hung low over thick thighs. In front of the class was a thin woman in glasses, as thin and flat-chested as her "pupils" were fat and broad. But there was no sign of Nancy.

He walked on and made his way to Peter Hynd's. Peter was down in the trench with his pickaxe. Above him stood Nancy with that awful dead-black hair of hers and her old-fashioned stiletto heels sinking into the earth. "Since you're that busy, I'll be off," he heard Nancy say mournfully.

Peter leaped out of the trench. He smiled down at her with that blinding smile of his. "Come later," he said, "when I'm not so busy." And then he kissed her on both cheeks, very warmly, each kiss close to either side of the nose. Nancy stared up at him, doting, almost sagging in his arms.

"Fine day," said Hamish in a loud voice.

Peter smiled. Nancy gave Hamish a look of pure loathing before tottering off.

"Is this a social call?" asked Peter.

"No," said Hamish curtly.

Peter looked amused. "We'd best go inside, but don't take too long. I've an awful lot to do."

They went into the kitchen. "Coffee?" asked Peter, holding up a thermos flask.

"No," said Hamish with the Highlander's innate dislike of taking any hospitality from someone he disliked, or, in the case of Peter, had come to dislike.

"So what brings you?" asked Peter, pouring himself a cup.

"I haff come to ask you to leave the women of Drim alone."

Peter looked at Hamish in amazement and then began to laugh.

"It is not the laughing matter," said Hamish. "I like a quiet life and I do not want any trouble on my beat."

"This is marvellous," crowed Peter. "Are you expecting a crime of passion?"

"Aye, maybe. This is not the south of England. People here know very well how to hate, and hate deeply."

For one moment, Peter seemed to lose years and looked almost like a sulky schoolboy being reprimanded by a teacher. But he turned the full force of his charm on Hamish. "Look, I admit my presence here has gone a bit to the heads of the ladies. But have you seen their men? Believe me, in a few weeks, the novelty will wear off and they'll no more notice me than one of their sheep."

"They'll lose interest all right chust so long as you do not continue to feed it," Hamish went doggedly on, although Peter was beginning to make him feel silly.

"You're worrying about nothing."

"Chust try to be as friendly with the men as you are with the women."

"Be reasonable. That's a bit difficult. They didn't want to know me from the beginning. All the offers of help came from the women."

"Try. It's a pity there isn't a pub here."

Peter grinned. "Oh, but there is."

"Where?"

"At the back of Jock Kennedy's after closing time. The minister frowns on all alcohol, and I would guess he's about the only person in Drim who does not know of its existence."

Hamish stood up. "Go carefully. The Highland temperament can be dangerous."

He walked back down to the village. If Jock Kennedy was running a pub without a licence, then it was his job to put a stop to it. But as he looked around the darkness of Drim, he decided to leave it to another day. The men needed their comforts.

He climbed into the Land Rover and sat back and thought about Peter Hynd, and then decided that Jimmy Macleod's distress had made him take the whole situation too seriously. One of the men would pick a fight with Peter sooner or later and give him a nasty time of it and then the Englishman would leave.

He closed his eyes, planning to have about ten minutes nap before going back to Lochdubh, lulled by the beat, beat, beat of the music from the community hall. And then, just as his eyes were closing, he saw something that made him open them wide. Peter Hynd was strolling towards the community centre. Hamish slowly climbed down from the car and made his way to the hall and looked in the window just as Peter Hynd strolled inside.

What a fluttering and cackling and fuss! It was just, he thought gloomily, like watching a rooster strut into the farmyard among the hens. Edie Aubrey switched off the music and fluttered up to Peter, who kissed her warmly on the cheek. Hamish turned away in disgust.

Over Edie's thin shoulder, Peter saw the policeman's cap disappearing from sight. "Do you want to stay and watch my little class?" asked Edie.

Peter turned and smiled at all the women. The door opened and Nancy Macleod came in, her eyes flashing this way and that. "No, I had better get on with my work," he said. "I was just passing and thought I'd drop in to say hello. That's a new outfit, isn't it,

Edie? Pink suits you."

Edie smiled at him mistily, feeling the money spent in Strathbane at the sports shop had been worth every penny. When he looked at her like that, she felt like Jane Fonda. Peter made his way to the door, a hug here, a kiss there, ending up with Nancy. "I've kissed you already," he teased and slid past her to the door. Nancy started after him with a lost look in her eyes.

Peter went back to his cottage highly pleased. He was glad Hamish had seen him. But Hamish needed to be punished. He flicked through the Highlands and Islands Telephone Directory until he found the Tommel Castle Hotel. He began to dial the number.

"I don't remember you," said Priscilla.

"I was in the other night," said Peter, "just before closing time. You warned me not to drink too much."

"Oh, yes, I remember you now."

"Look, I feel like a decent meal and I've heard that Italian restaurant in Lochdubh is pretty good. Like to join me for dinner?"

"It's very kind of you, but —"

"I saw Hamish in Drim this afternoon. Looks like he's going to be here all day."

"What is he doing there?" Priscilla's voice was sharp.

"Just sloping about talking to the locals. I want a bit of company at dinner, Priscilla. It's not like a date. I know you're engaged to Hamish."

"Oh, very well. What time?"

"Eight suit you?"

"Fine."

"See you then. 'Bye."

Priscilla replaced the receiver. Why had she done that? Well, to be honest, she was furious with Hamish. It was quite clear to her that he had gone to Drim simply to get out of house-hunting. And the house outside Strathbane had been perfect, situated on a rise, good garden, airy rooms, nothing like that poky police station. She experienced a stab of conscience, which was telling her that she should leave Hamish Macbeth's character alone and not try to change him. But her father had raged about the proposed marriage and had told Priscilla that Hamish Macbeth was a layabout who would never come to anything, and Priscilla was hell-bent on proving her father wrong.

Hamish felt in a mellow mood when he returned to Lochdubh. He could not help contrasting his own village favourably with

Drim. The little white houses faced the loch. There was an openness and friendliness about the place. The air was clear and light, with that pearly light of northern Scotland where the nights are hardly ever dark in the summer. A sea-gull skimmed the loch, its head turning this way and that, looking for fish; a seal rolled and turned as lazily as any Mediterranean bather; people stood at their garden gates, talking in soft Highland voices; and the hum and chatter of the diners in the Italian restaurant came to Hamish's ears, reminding him that he was hungry.

To make amends to Priscilla, he went into the police station and phoned her. He was told she was out and settled back to wait. If Priscilla was "out," it meant she was headed in his direction. But as the hands of the clock crept around and his stomach rumbled, he realized that Priscilla must have gone somewhere else. He decided to treat himself to a meal at the Italian restaurant. He ambled along. As he drew nearer, he saw a couple sitting at the front window of the restaurant, noticed the gleam of candle-light on blonde hair, and saw with a stab of shock that Priscilla was having dinner with Peter Hynd. Hamish stood like a heron in a pool, one foot raised, arrested in mid-air.

Then he slowly turned and began to walk back the way he had come.

CHAPTER 3

A man that studieth revenge keeps his own wounds green.

Francis Bacon

Had Hamish been a Lowland Scot, he would have confronted Priscilla and Peter, or, at least, have phoned her later to tell her what he thought of her. But he was Highland, and his vanity was deeply wounded. So, maliciously hell-bent on mischief, he drove up to the Tommel Castle Hotel.

The first welcome sight that met his eyes was a new receptionist, a small, pretty girl with a cheeky face and a mop of auburn curls.

He had seen her before. She had, he judged, started work at the hotel about a fortnight ago. He smiled at her and said, "Where's Priscilla?"

"She's gone out," said the receptionist.

"Can I help? Och, I'm being silly. You're Hamish."

"You're Scottish," exclaimed Hamish. "I thought only the English took jobs as receptionists in Highland hotels. Are you from these parts?"

"No, from Perth." She held out a small hand. "Sophy Bisset."

"Well, Sophy Bisset, are you on duty for long tonight?"

She glanced at the clock. "Harry, the night porter, should be here any moment to relieve me."

"Fancy a bite of dinner?"

Her bright grey eyes twinkled at him. "I thought you lot had your dinner in the middle of the day and your tea by five."

"I've been working hard."

"As a matter of fact, I've only had a sandwich since lunch-time. Oh, here's Harry."

"Come along and I'll stand ye dinner at that Italian place."

She looked amused, as if at some private joke, but she picked up her handbag and said cheerfully, "All right. Let's go."

Seated in the Land Rover, she said, "This is very kind of you, Hamish. Safe in the arms of the law."

"Chust so," said Hamish, throwing her a

slanting look. Had there been a mocking edge to her voice?

Wishing he were not wearing his uniform, Hamish ushered her into the restaurant. "Oh, there's Priscilla. Surprise, surprise," said Sophy, and Hamish at once knew that Sophy had been perfectly aware that they would meet Priscilla and her date. Willie Lamont, Hamish's ex-policeman, came bustling up in his waiter's uniform of striped sweater and indecently tight trousers. "Tch, Willie," admonished Hamish. "If you go around in breeks like that, someone will be pinching your bum."

"Lucia made me wear them," said Willie sulkily. Lucia was his Italian wife. "Are you going to join Priscilla?"

"We'll chust sit at this wee table in the corner."

Willie handed them menus and sailed off.

Hamish looked at Sophy over the top of his menu. "You knew Priscilla was here," he accused.

Sophy nodded, her eyes dancing. "The only reason a man like you would ask me out, Hamish Macbeth, would be to get revenge on Priscilla. I mean, just look at her. She could have stepped out of the pages of *Vogue*."

There was simple admiration in her voice.

Hamish reluctantly lowered the menu and looked at his beloved. She was wearing a white frilly blouse with a plunging neckline and a short, tight black skirt. The bell of her golden hair shone in the candle-light. She threw back her head and laughed at something Peter was saying.

"Look at me instead," ordered Sophy. "She's not enjoying herself one bit."

"Could've have fooled me," grumbled Hamish. Willie came back and took their orders.

Priscilla was not enjoying herself. Before Hamish had come in, she had been about to leave. At first it had been nice to be out with such an attractive and charming man, but Priscilla was conscious of Willie the waiter's disapproving stares and of the cold looks she was getting from several of the villagers at the other tables, who obviously felt that she should not be out with another man. Then there was something about Peter that repelled her. She sensed in him a calculating hardness, and when he talked about meeting Hamish that afternoon, Priscilla became perfectly sure Peter had asked her out just to spite Hamish, although Peter did not tell her what Hamish had said. At last she gathered up her handbag and said, "Thank you for a lovely evening. I'll have a word with Hamish before I go."

Before Peter could say anything, she sailed over to Hamish's table. "Good evening," said Priscilla sweetly. "Finished your work, Sophy?"

"Yes, Harry's on duty."

"Did you give the Dunsters in room twenty-five their bill?"

"Yes, they paid and will leave in the morning."

"And did the Trents arrive?"

"Just after you left. They're in room fourteen."

"And did you —"

"For heffen's sake," said Hamish Macbeth loudly and crossly. "Leave the girl be, Priscilla. She's not on duty now."

"Then the pair of you should get on very well," snapped Priscilla. "When were you last on duty, Hamish? And don't give me that crap about investigating in Drim. You just wanted to get out of house-hunting."

Peter fidgeted behind Priscilla. Things were not working out as he had planned. He was on the outside while, it appeared, two attractive women were competing for the attentions of Hamish.

"Priscilla, we'll talk about this later," said Hamish. "Now can I get on wi' my dinner?"

Priscilla turned on her heel and marched

out. She suddenly remembered the seer's prediction, turned firmly to Peter and shook his hand heartily. "All the very best in Drim," said Priscilla briskly and walked away quickly to her own car, which was parked on the waterfront.

Despite his uneasiness that he had gone too far, Hamish enjoyed Sophy's company and her amusing tales of working in hotels in Glasgow and Perth. When he ran her back to the hotel and said good night to her, he debated with himself whether to call on Priscilla and then decided against it. *He* was the injured party.

Morning brought regret. Panic began to set in. He forgot bossy and managing Priscilla and only remembered his dear Watson of previous cases. There was a knock at the kitchen door. He opened it and saw Priscilla standing there. She smiled. She held out her hand. She said, "Truce?" He gathered her in his arms and kissed her until his toes curled.

She finally released herself. "You're not getting off that easily, Hamish Macbeth. Come along. We're going to look at that house."

And at that moment, Hamish would have agreed to anything. They drove off in Priscilla's car, Towser in the back seat, fitful sunlight chasing across the moors, and the wind heavy with the sweet scent of heather. Hamish did not speak about Sophy, and Priscilla did not mention Peter.

His sunny mood lasted until they turned in at the short drive leading to the house. It was a Victorian villa, neat and compact. It looked down on the bleak high-rises of Strathbane.

"I kept the key," said Priscilla gaily. "Just wait until you see this."

Hamish followed her in, with Towser at his heels. He stood in the hall and looked around. On one side lay a living-room, on the other a dining-room. "Come in here and look at the view," carolled Priscilla from the living-room.

He went in and stood with his hands in his pockets. He gave a little shiver. "This is an evil house."

Priscilla swung round from the window and stared. "Stop fooling about, Hamish."

"I am not being funny, Priscilla. This is a sad house. Something bad happened here."

"You mean someone died here?" Priscilla looked at him scornfully, her hands on her hips. "Of course they did. The place is at least a hundred years old. Come and see the kitchen."

"I'll wait for you outside," said Hamish.

She darted to the doorway and blocked his exit.

"Listen to me, I am not falling for that bad-vibes Highland nonsense. This is a perfectly good house."

"Who is the owner?"

"I don't know. I don't care either. Just look at the kitchen, Hamish. That'll make you change your mind."

He shrugged. "Okay."

She walked through to the back, where a large square kitchen lay. It was airy and light, with a primrose-coloured Aga cooker and plenty of cupboards and shelves. Hamish looked about and then said, "I've had enough. I've got to get outside."

Priscilla followed him out, her face tight with anger. "You are determined not to move to Strathbane. You are determined to stay in Lochdubh and rot."

"Humour me," he said. "You've got to take that key back to the estate agent, right? Just let me ask who lived here."

She walked in silence to the car and he got in beside her. Towser, sensing the bad atmosphere, crouched down on the back seat.

"Why did you buy that cooker for the police station if you had no intention of living there?" asked Hamish at last.

The correct answer to that was that somewhere deep inside, Priscilla was perfectly sure she would never budge Hamish Macbeth, but she would not admit that even to herself.

"You need one," she said curtly.

Strathbane swallowed them up with its mean streets and perpetual air of failure, a sort of inner city transferred to the north of Scotland. Oily water heaved in the harbour and the rusting hulk of a ship listed on its side. Sea-gulls screamed mournfully. Priscilla parked in a multi-storey and they walked down to Strathbane's new shopping precinct called The Highlander's Welcome. It was cobbled in round fake cobbles of an orange colour and set about with plastic palms whose leaves clattered mournfully in the damp breeze from the sea. Small round women in the Strathbane uniform of track suit and jogging trousers struggled with plastic bags of shopping. Men stood in groups, smoking moodily and occasionally spitting viciously at nothing in particular.

Priscilla led the way into the estate agent's. A young man rushed forward. "Everything satisfactory?" he asked, taking the key from Priscilla.

"We're still making up our minds," said Priscilla.

"Who owns it?" asked Hamish.

"That's confidential," said the young man quickly, fearing that Hamish meant to go behind his back and make some sort of private deal. "I have another property here, Miss Halburton-Smythe." The young man pulled out a folder. While Priscilla bent her head over it, Hamish's eyes ranged around the office and fell on a typist at a desk by the window. She looked up and Hamish winked at her. She grinned and patted her hair.

"Maybe another day," said Priscilla, straightening up.

Once outside, Hamish said, "I'll stay on in Strathbane for a bit."

"What? How are you going to get home?"

"I'll hitch a lift."

"You're determined to stay here and ferret about looking for non-existent criminals who once lived in that house." Priscilla was becoming angry. "Suit yourself. You should wake up to the fact that you are hell-bent on refusing promotion."

"Maybe it iss you yourself who should wake up to that fact."

Priscilla strode off without a backward look and Hamish looked after her miserably. He then remembered Towser was still in the car. But Priscilla would take Towser home.

He hung about the estate agent's, discreetly hidden by a plastic palm until he saw the typist emerging for her lunch. He hurried over and bumped into her as if by accident. "Sorry," said Hamish, and then affected surprise. "Aren't you that pretty girl I saw in the estate agent's a while ago?"

Her pasty face turned up to his and she giggled. "That's me."

"I'm Hamish Macbeth."

"Tracey McWhirter," she said.

"Tell you what, Tracey, I wass chust on my way to that coffee shop for a sandwich or something. Care to join me?"

She giggled again but nodded and fell into step beside him, tottering on her high heels. After he had bought her a coffee and a Highlandman's Lunch, a wad of dry French bread with limp lettuce and smoked mackerel, Hamish said, "I was up at that house this morning." He hoped she had not heard him asking the young man for the name of the owner. "That was George Emming's place, wasn't it?"

"Oh, no," said Tracey guilelessly. She paused to brush crumbs from her T-shirt, which was surprisingly sophisticated in that it bore no legend at all. "That's Mr. Hendry, the teacher's, place."

"Oh, him that teaches English at Strathbane High?"

"Chemistry."

"Ah."

"And what do you do yourself, Mr. Macbeth?"

"Hamish, I'm a civil servant." Hamish was not in uniform.

"On the council?"

"Something like that."

"Do you work for Miss Halburton-Smythe?"

Hamish winced slightly at the innocent assumption that he could not be on any social level with Priscilla. But he did not want Tracey to think he had taken her for coffee merely to get information from her, so he said vaguely, "We both live in Lochdubh."

"I'm glad I don't live in a place like that," said Tracey. "I mean, what is there to do?"

"We have fun," said Hamish defensively. "We have the ceilidhs."

"Oh, them," Tracey snorted dismissively. "Big fat woman thumping around in the eightsome reel and wee men outside passing half-bottles o' whisky to each other. We have discos in Strathbane."

"How can you bear all that thumping music and those strobe lights giving folks epileptic fits?" demanded Hamish.

"Oh, well, someone of your age wouldn't understand," said Tracey with all the tolerance of eighteen looking at thirty-something.

Feeling a hundred-year-old peasant, Hamish left Tracey and made his way on foot to Strathbane High School. It was a huge barracks of a place, built of red brick in the thirties, set among rain-washed playing fields where sea-gulls squatted on the grass. Children were returning to their classes after lunch. He stopped one boy and asked for the headmaster's office, was corrected and told it was the head *teacher* and pointed in the right direction. The head teacher was a woman who introduced herself as Beth Dublin. She was a small, mousy creature who looked about the same age as Tracey but must have been a good bit older. To Hamish's request to see the chemistry teacher, Mr. Hendry, she said that he had a free period and could be found in the staff common-room and she would take him there. On the way along a gloomy corridor smelling of stale cigarette smoke and disinfectant, Beth said, "His kids aren't in trouble again, are they?"

Startled, Hamish wondered at first if she had guessed he was a policeman and then decided she probably thought he might be an irate parent. "Not that I know of," he said cautiously. "Are they often in trouble?"

She primmed her lips and then said, "That's not for me to say."

She opened the door of the staff common-room and a fog of cigarette smoke rolled out. They may dash the weed from your lips in New York and frown on you in London, but the north of Scotland is the last hope of the tobacco companies outside the Third World. "Mr. Hendry?" called Beth. A small man with a large head and a scrubbing-brush hair-style appeared in the gloom. "Visitor," said Beth and left Hamish to it.

"I am Hamish Macbeth, Mr. Hendry," said Hamish. "My fiancée and I have just been to see your house, the one for sale."

"Come over to the window where we can talk," said Mr. Hendry eagerly. "It's a grand house and you're getting a good offer. It would have been snapped up long ago if it weren't for this damn recession."

They sat down in chairs by the window. The other teachers were leaving for their classes and soon Mr. Hendry and Hamish were alone.

"My fiancée," lied Hamish, "is a verra

72

superstitious lady and she would not like to be staying anywhere there's been a violent death or murder."

"Nothing like that," he said quickly. "We bought it fifteen years ago from a couple who emigrated to Australia, and what happened to the people before that I don't know, but if there had been a murder or anything like that, I would have heard of it."

"My fiancée said she felt bad vibes in the house."

"Och, you Highlanders," said Mr. Hendry, who was a Lowland Scot, "you're always thinking you've got the second sight and you're psychic. All havers."

"I wouldna' say it's all havers," said Hamish crossly. "We haven't made up our minds."

"If you want my wife to take you around and show your lady where everything is in the kitchen," he said, "she'd be glad to do it."

"Well, my fiancée's gone back home. But if Mrs. Hendry could spare the time . . ."

"Wait there. Got your car with you?"

"No, I'm on foot."

"I'll get her to pick you up."

Mrs. Hendry turned out to be a sedate middle-aged woman with pepper-and-salt hair, a tweed suit, a thick energetic body, and tiny plump feet encased in brogues. Hamish was beginning to feel very silly indeed as she drove him competently back out to the house. He noticed this time that it was called Craigallen. He listened patiently as she opened cupboards and pointed to electric points. She then took him round the garden. "It was a happy house for us," she said, "and I hope you'll be happy as well. Oh, would you look at those weeds!"

She crouched down over a flower-bed and stretched out a plump, beringed hand to pluck a weed. As she did so, her sleeve fell back. Hamish stared down at a vicious purple bruise on her wrist. As if aware of his gaze, she tugged down her sleeve.

He promised to return and asked her to drop him in the centre of Strathbane. He ambled into the police headquarters and made his way to the records room, where he asked if the police had ever been called out to a house called Craigallen on the Lochdubh Road. After the dragon in charge had made him sign multiple bureaucratic forms, she produced a slim file.

The police had been called out two years ago. Craigallen was pretty isolated, but a man walking his dog had reported screams and shouts. The police had called but the Hendrys said they had been watching a noisy video.

Hamish scowled down at it. What if Hendry was a wife-beater? And why had the head teacher assumed that something had been wrong with his children? He gave a little sigh. It was really none of his business. Probably Priscilla was right and he had only done it to get out of moving to Strathbane. And it was a long road home without transport and he had missed the one daily bus to Lochdubh.

He left the police headquarters and saw a familiar figure across the road . . . Edie Aubrey. He walked over to her and introduced himself. "I was hoping to get a lift back or part of the way," said Hamish.

"I can take you as far as Drim," said Edie, blinking up at him through her thick spectacles. "Maybe one of the locals will be going to Lochdubh. Harry Baxter should be setting out for the night's fishing."

"Grand," said Hamish. "Finished your messages?"

She nodded. She was carrying a plastic shopping bag labelled "Naughties," which Hamish knew was Strathbane's newest lingerie shop, having previously studied the delicate items in the window and wondered who bought them, as the washing-lines from Strathbane to Lochdubh were hung with sturdier and more serviceable items.

When they were driving out of Strathbane, Hamish said, "Peter Hynd seems to have caused quite a flutter."

"Such a charming boy," enthused Edie. "Before he came, I kept telling them they ought to exercise, but nothing would get them started. Now they're all at my classes every day."

"Good for you," said Hamish. He added maliciously, "It's a pity there are no young lassies in Drim for him to marry."

There was a startled silence and then Edie said, "Och, well, he says to me the other day, he says, 'I can't be doing with these young women, Edie,' he says. 'Give me a mature woman every time.'"

"And has he any particular mature woman in mind?"

Edie giggled and batted her sparse eyelashes. "That would be telling."

Hamish guessed that the perfidious Peter had somehow led every woman in Drim to think she was the favoured one. He shivered. It was all an amusing game to Peter, but a dangerous one to play in a shut-off village in the Highlands of Scotland.

Edie chattered on about the improvements that Peter was making to the croft house all the long road to Drim until Hamish was glad to be dropped outside Harry Baxter's cottage and escape from her.

A waif-like child was sitting outside, staring at nothing with those light-grey Highland eyes. Hamish held out his hand and introduced himself. She gave it a shake. "I'm Heather," she said solemnly. Hamish judged her to be about twelve years old. "Are your ma and da at home?" asked Hamish.

"Ma's at home. Da's sleeping."

"I'll chust see your ma." Hamish edged past the little girl whose steady stare unnerved him. Betty Baxter was in the kitchen, her coarse, dyed-blonde hair piled up on her head, her normally swarthy gypsy features covered in thick white foundation cream. "I came to see if your man could give me a lift to Lochdubh when he's going to the fishing," said Hamish.

"Aye. I'm sure he could," said Betty. "Like some tea? I'm about to get Harry up fur his."

"That's verra kind of you."

"Sit yourself doon." She crossed to the doorway and shouted up the stairs. "Harry! Tea!"

After a few moments, Harry shuffled in, unwashed, unshaved, and with his braces hanging down over his baggy trousers.

Hamish felt a stab of irritation. What did the men of Drim expect if they went around looking like this?

Tea was "high tea," consisting of fish and chips, strong tea and a pile of bread and butter. After Hamish had repeated his request for a lift and had been told he could get one, the three ate in silence.

"Doesn't your daughter eat with you?" asked Hamish.

"Oh, her," said Betty with a massive shrug. "She'll come in when she's hungry."

When they had finished, Harry hitched up his braces, wiped his mouth with the back of his hand, and pulled on his boots and put on his oilskins. "Wait ootside in the truck, Hamish," he said. "Won't be long."

Hamish went out and sat in the passenger seat and rolled down the window. The voices came clearly from the house.

"You are not to go doon tae the ceilidh tonight," came Harry's voice.

"I'll go anywhere I like!" Betty's, shrill and contemptuous.

"Ach, you're all making a damn fool o' yourselves over a bit o' a lad who's laughing up his sleeve at the lot o' ye. Anyway, ye havenae a hope in hell. Ailsa Kennedy, Jock's wife, was seen leaving his cottage last night at two in the morning."

"That's a lie!" Betty, panting with outrage.
Hamish turned his head slightly and saw
young Heather. She was sitting on the grass,
with her slight figure pressed against the
walls of the cottage. Hamish climbed down
from the truck.

"Are you coming, Harry?" he shouted
loudly and angrily. "And wee Heather's out
here and could do with a bite to eat."

There was a sudden silence, and then
Harry came out at a rush, his face red.

He climbed in the truck and Hamish hurriedly jumped into the passenger seat.

It was a silent journey to Lochdubh,
Harry hurtling round the bends at ferocious
speed as if trying to put as much distance
between himself and his wife as quickly as
possible. Hamish thought gloomily that, for
his own peace of mind, he should leave the
village of Drim alone. But there was the
question of the illegal "pub" that Jock
Kennedy was running. Conscience and duty
told him he would have to do something
about it. But not now.

After Harry dropped him off, he took his
own transport and went to the Tommel
Castle Hotel. Towser was there in Sophy's
care because, he learned, Priscilla had
driven down to Inverness to visit friends.
What friends? he wondered, feeling de-

pressed. He imagined a large house outside Inverness containing some wealthy and eligible son, some *successful* eligible son.

Sophy regarded his downcast face with bright amusement. "Do you know," she said, "I think this might be a good evening to take *you* for dinner. What about that Italian restaurant again?"

"Why not?" said Hamish ungraciously. "See you there at eight. I've got things to do."

He returned to the police station and fed a delighted Towser, who was a greedy dog and had already been generously fed by Priscilla before she left for Inverness. With reluctance, he washed and changed and set out for the Italian restaurant.

"Getting to be a regular," commented Willie Lamont. "Miss Halburton-Smythe likes the window table."

"I am not dining with Priscilla."

"Then sit anywhere," said Willie sourly.

Hamish sighed. No one in Lochdubh was going to like his having dinner with Sophy twice, and by tomorrow the whole of Lochdubh would know about it and that included Priscilla. Sophy came in. She was wearing a pink sweater and a tweed skirt. She looked fresh and wholesome and uncomplicated. Hamish was glad she had not dressed up.

Priscilla, he thought disloyally, always dressed up when she was out for dinner, even at this local restaurant. But his real reason for being glad was a cowardly one. A dressed-up Sophy would have made it look more like a date.

"How was the house?" asked Sophy, after they had placed their orders.

Hamish did not even bother to ask how she knew he had been house-hunting. Living in the Highlands meant getting used to everyone knowing what one did and where one went.

"I didn't like it," he said. "No, Willie, I don't need to taste the wine. It'll be the same as last night."

"Not much of a wine connoisseur, are you?" said Willie. "Wine varies from bottle tae bottle."

"But not in giant flagons of Bulgarian red, which is what you filled these decanters from. I've seen the kitchens."

"Och, you're a right downer," said Willie unrepentantly.

"Why didn't you like the house?" asked Sophy.

"You'll think this silly . . . bad vibes."

"No, I don't think it silly at all, Hamish. Some houses have a bad atmosphere."

"Aye, but I carried things a wee bit too

81

far. I left Priscilla and went off to find the owners. It appears to me that the husband's a bit of a wife-beater. Not verra dramatic."

"Oh, but something should be done about it. Think of the children."

"But I cannae do anything about it. Nothing can be done about it unless the wife puts in a complaint."

"Then you should encourage her to make one!"

"I'll see. But it's difficult. Strathbane and what happens there is really nothing to do with me."

"I suppose not," said Sophy. "Oh, I gather that beautiful young man who was here last night with Priscilla is living over at Drim, of all places."

"Yes," said Hamish sourly, "and I wish to God he weren't."

"Jealous, Hamish?"

"Of him and Priscilla? No, Priscilla's not daft. The situation is this. He's been making passes at the middle-aged women of Drim and it's fair turned their heads. They're all titivating themselves — hair dye, exercise classes, fancy underwear . . ."

"How do you know about the underwear?" teased Sophy.

"I found one of them with a shopping bag from Naughties, that new lingerie shop."

"Surely it's all harmless. If he flirts with all of them, then no single one need feel dangerously jealous."

"This is not Perth," said Hamish haughtily, as if Perth lay in the south of England instead of just outside the Highland line in central Scotland. "The men are brooding and they'll become violent."

"Well, so one of them'll give him a sock on the nose and he'll take himself off."

Hamish shook his head. "I smell trouble."

" 'By the pricking of my thumbs, something wicked this way comes'?"

"Something like that."

The ceilidh in the community hall was in full swing. Ailsa Kennedy was dancing the Dashing White Sergeant with Peter Hynd. She had fiery-red hair — undyed — and an aggressive bosom, thrusting breasts which seemed to point accusingly. Her waist was slim, and her hips, under her swinging skirts, broad. She had very piercing bright-blue eyes, which this evening were filled with laughter as Peter twirled her about. Jock Kennedy leaned against a pillar and watched moodily, his great arms crossed across his barrel of a chest. Then he suddenly detached himself from the pillar and went outside into the pearly-white light of the northern Scottish evening and joined a group of men who were passing around a bottle of whisky.

"We wass chust deciding what to do about him in there," said the crofter Jimmy Macleod with a jerk of his head.

"The Sassenach?" said Jock. "I feel like bashing his head in."

The men gathered around him, small men, angry men, crabbed and bitter men. "Aye, do it, Jock," they said. And one voice, louder than the others, said, "I'll call him out here for a dram and you let him have it."

Jock began to smile. "Aye, get him out here. It's time that yin had a taste o' Highland hospitality."

The women saw Peter being approached, saw him led to the door. "I'm goin' too," said Betty Baxter to Ailsa Kennedy. "They're up to something out there."

The two women went outside and then Betty began to scream, for Jock Kennedy was rolling up his sleeves and saying, "It's time you had a thrashing."

The dancers began to crowd out and soon a circle was formed around the two men, the women crying and screaming that Peter would be killed.

Jock moved in, his great fists swinging.

Peter dodged every blow, moving like lightning, while Jock lumbered around, swinging punches. Then Peter's foot shot out in a karate kick and the kick landed fairly and squarely and with great force on Jock Kennedy's balls. He let out a groan and rolled over, retching, on the ground.

"You asked for it," said Peter lightly, and surrounded by a coterie of admiring and excited women, he went back into the dance-hall.

Heather Baxter moved slowly out of the shadows, her little face white. Her best party dress fluttering in the pale light, she moved away from the community hall in the direction of home, as light and silent as a moth, her feet making no sound on the grass.

CHAPTER 4

He speaks the kindest words, and looks
    such things,
Vows with so much passion, swears with
    so much grace,
That 'tis a kind of Heaven to be deluded
    by him.

                       Nathaniel Lee

Priscilla received a phone call from Susan Daviot right after she had learned that Hamish Macbeth had been seen having dinner with Sophy the night before.

"It's quait near Craigallen," fluted Mrs. Daviot. "Ever so naice and a reel snip, Priscilla. I have the aid conference today at the town hall, but if you and Hamish would like to see it, ai'll give you the instructions."

Priscilla took them down. She had no intention of doing anything about seeing another house. Why irritate Hamish further?

But when she replaced the receiver her father came into the office and stood watching her, rocking a little on his heels. "How did you get on at the Frasers' last night?" he asked.

"Fine," said Priscilla. "Pleasant evening."

"Was John Fraser there?"

"Yes, he was home for a few days."

"Now that's a fellow you should be thinking about. Successful stockbroker. When I think that my only daughter should be even contemplating throwing herself away on a layabout of a Highlander —"

"That's enough," said Priscilla sharply. "Who solved all those cases which baffled Strathbane? Who . . . ?"

"And who is such a lazy poacher that he refuses promotion?"

"Hamish will be a chief superintendent one of these days."

"Rubbish!"

Priscilla picked up her notes and made for the door. "Stop criticizing Hamish, Pa, it doesn't have the slightest effect on me."

But it did. Somehow, she found herself driving to the police station, more determined than ever to shake Hamish out of this village and into success.

Hamish was feeding his hens. His face lit up with all the old gladness when he saw her, and then a shuttered look came over his eyes when they fell on the notes in her hand.

"You've found another house," he said.

"Look, it wouldn't do any harm to look at it, Hamish. Enjoy your dinner last night?"

"Aye, it was grand."

"As your fiancée, I feel I should ask you your intentions towards Sophy Bisset."

"My intentions are about evening the score. She asked me out, not the other way round, and since you had gone off to Inverness without even phoning . . ."

"I did phone, but you weren't back. What did you find out?"

"It seems the owner of Craigallen is a wife-beater."

"And you know that for a fact?"

"Not exactly."

Priscilla sighed. "Let's just look at this house, Hamish. We want somewhere decent to bring up our children."

His eyes gleamed with malice. "Aye, children would be fine. Know anything about how to go about getting some, Priscilla?"

"Hamish! Are you coming to see this house or not?"

"On one condition, we call in at Drim on the road back."

"Why?"

"Jock Kennedy's running an illegal pub at the back of his shop. Now I know about it, I've got to put a stop to it."

"All right."

"I'll drive, as we're going on police business sometime today. Down, Towser," for Towser was standing on his hind legs with his muddy paws on Priscilla's skirt.

"He doesn't bother me," said Priscilla. "We'll take him with us."

Hamish felt weak at the knees. It was the occasional contrast between Priscilla's cool beauty and her lack of concern at being pawed by the smelly and doting Towser that made him fall in love with her all over again. He pushed Towser aside and pulled her into his arms, but she said, "Your neighbour's watching us." He felt his spirits plunge again. He could not have given a damn at that moment who was watching them. He wished with all his heart that Priscilla would lose her reserve. He had a sudden vivid memory of Willie Lamont when he was engaged to Lucia, hugging and kissing her and then noticing a group of grinning villagers. He had said something to the beautiful Lucia and she had laughed and put an arm about his waist and, with her head on his shoulder, they had gone into the restaurant. He began to become very angry indeed with Priscilla. He *deserved* someone a bit warmer and less managing. Priscilla sensed his change of mood as she climbed into the Land Rover. She had an impulse to put her hand on his arm, to say, "Let's forget it," but she remembered her father's angry and contemptuous face and remained silent.

As they were approaching Craigallen, Priscilla said, "Care for another look, Hamish?"

He shook his head, but as they were driving slowly past, he saw Mrs. Hendry in the garden and slowed to a stop. "Well, maybe, just a quick look around the outside."

As soon as Priscilla saw Mrs. Hendry, she realized the reason for Hamish's odd enthusiasm to see a house he loathed. She wanted to tell him to forget it, but Mrs. Hendry was already rising to her feet from weeding a flower-bed. "How nice to see you again," she said to Hamish. "Come into the house. I was just about to make a cup of tea."

Priscilla opened her mouth to protest but Hamish had leaped forward. "I would chust love the cup of tea," he chattered, following Mrs. Hendry into the house and not even looking round to see if Priscilla was following them.

"I was upset at the state of the garden,"

said Mrs. Hendry. "You can't get good workers these days. Is there any hope you will buy the house?" She gave an awkward little laugh. "My husband thinks it's all my fault that we can't sell the place, but there you are, that's men for you. Always need someone to blame."

"Isn't that the case?" agreed Hamish, avoiding Priscilla's eye. "Why, the number o' cases of wife-beating I've seen because the man has to take any bad luck out on the woman."

"Really, Mr. Macbeth," said Mrs. Hendry. "I hope you are not suggesting my husband beats me!"

Hamish raised his hands in horror. "Did I say such a thing? Och, no, it's just that I am a policeman, Mrs. Hendry."

"Really?" She fiddled noisily with the cups.

"And the hell some women put up with, you chust wouldna' believe. And when I've said to them, 'Take the man to court,' they chust look at me blankly and say, 'He's done nothing wrong. Besides, I've got the children.' And there *are* the children growing up warped and miserable."

Mrs. Hendry dropped the kettle. Boiling water spilled all over the kitchen floor.

Priscilla took a cloth from the draining-board. "No, leave it," said Mrs. Hendry shrilly. "Leave it! I have not been sleeping well lately and my nerves are bad. I am sorry. But you had better go."

"Come along, Hamish," said Priscilla. "Are you sure you don't want me to help you clear up this mess, Mrs. Hendry?"

She shook her head.

Hamish and Priscilla went silently outside. As they drove off, Hamish cleared his throat and said, "Nothing can be done unless she wishes it done."

"Exactly," agreed Priscilla. "Turn off here to the left, Hamish. The house we want to see is called Haven. A few hundred yards along on the right. The owners are Mr. and Mrs. Peterman."

Hamish parked outside. The house was low and square, built, he guessed, sometime in the thirties. The garden was neat with regimented flowers and plants, evenly spaced, as if the distances between them had been measured by a ruler.

It was a one-storey house, the roof slate, the walls pebble-dashed, and the door had a top pane of stained glass. Priscilla rang the imitation ship's bell outside the door. A thin, nervous woman answered it. Her shoulders were hunched and her arms were hanging straight down and her head was jutting forward, as if someone had thrust a coat-hanger into her sweater. She had a long fringe down to her eyebrows and slate-coloured eyes stared out from under it. She was wearing skin-tight jeans and baseball boots.

"Good morning," said Priscilla. "We have come to see the house. Mrs. Peterman?"

"Yes." The woman held out a hand in welcome. The skin was red and glazed and the knuckles swollen.

"I am Priscilla Halburton-Smythe, and this is Hamish Macbeth, my fiancé."

"Pleased to meet you." She had a slight Yorkshire accent. "I'll take you around," she said. "There's one thing I will say, this house is always clean. You could eat off the floor. We'll start with the lounge."

The lounge, of which she was obviously very proud, contained a mushroom-coloured, three-piece suite which looked as if it had never been sat on. Despite the days of hair oil being long gone, both chairs and sofa were decorated with antimacassars. An electric fire of fake logs decorated the hearth in front of a pink-tiled fireplace. There was a low coffee-table in front of the sofa set about with coasters decorated with flamenco dancers. Against one wall was a hi-fi unit, and over the fireplace, a picture of a mountain scene painted by an amateur, all eye-hurting colours and peculiar perspective. The air was cold and stale. "And now the dining-room," said Mrs. Peterman, charging out, her shoulders hunched and her arms straight out like a character in a cheap cartoon where the animator had been trying to save on animation.

Priscilla and Hamish stood together, looking at a long dining-table surrounded by ladder-back chairs with petit-point cushions in such vile colours that Hamish suspected Mrs. Peterman had been responsible for them. There was a side-board of the kind called Swedish, a depressingly geometric thing. Outside, the wind of Sutherland rose in its usual violent, unheralded way, making this box of a place appear to Hamish a temporary excrescence on the Highland landscape of moorland and mountain which lay beyond the "picture windows."

"Don't you have the central heating?" he said, looking around.

"We have electric-storage heaters," said Mrs. Peterman, "but we only use the heaters in winter. Too much heat makes you soft. The kitchen's through here behind the dining-room."

The kitchen was full of those gleaming white units bought from a Do-It-Yourself shop. The floor of black-and-white linoleum tiles shone brightly enough to hurt the eyes. A square plastic-topped table and four metal kitchen chairs with plastic seats dominated the centre. "We'll be taking the fridge and the cooker," said Mrs. Peterman. Priscilla was for once at a loss for anything to say. She wanted to escape. But there were still the bedrooms to see, two of them, one single and one double. The double bedroom had twin beds, narrow and rigid, separated by a bedside table which held a large Bible. On the wall above the beds was a text: THOU GOD SEEST ME!

"The guest bedroom," said Mrs. Peterman, throwing open another door. They both looked bleakly at a cell of a room.

"Well, that's all very nice," said Priscilla brightly. "We'll let you know. We have several other places to see."

"You'll not see one better than this," she said. "We've just put it on the market. Not like them at Craigallen. They've had that place up for sale for a year."

Hamish hesitated on the doorstep. "Charming woman, Mrs. Hendry."

"Oh, her? The things that woman puts up with."

"What things?"

Her mouth closed like a trap. "I do not

discuss my neighbours."

"Well, that's that," said Hamish with a sigh of relief as he drove off. "Don't tell me you want to live in a place like that, Priscilla."

"No, it was pretty dire," she said. "But Craigallen is all right, Hamish."

"A bad house," said Hamish firmly. "Let's go to Drim."

"Do you know," said Priscilla, "that in all the time I've lived up here, I've never been to Drim. I've heard it's a dead-alive sort of place."

"Aye, it's all of that."

They drove down towards Drim. Below them they could see the black sheen of water on the loch, that thin sea loch which lay between the towering walls of the mountains where nothing grew in the scree on the flanks except an occasional stunted tree. As they climbed down from the car, the air was heavy and still. Either the wind had suddenly dropped, thought Priscilla, or Drim was so protected from the elements that hardly a breath of air stirred the black waters of the loch.

"Why would anyone want to live here?" asked Priscilla, looking around.

Hamish shrugged. "Why would anyone want to live in a place like Strathbane either,

Priscilla? You'd best wait here. I'll see Jock on my own."

After Hamish had disappeared into the shop, the women began to emerge from the community hall after their exercise class. They stopped short at the sight of Priscilla standing beside the police Land Rover. She was wearing a short blue skirt of soft wool and a short-sleeved wool sweater. A white cashmere cardigan was draped about her shoulders. Her long legs in sheer stockings ended in low-heeled, tan leather court shoes. The women huddled together and stared at her from the top of her smooth blonde head to the tips of her shoes.

"What's someone like that doing here?" asked Betty Baxter harshly.

"Maybe she's come tae see Peter," said Nancy Macleod, voicing all their worries.

"In a polis car?" demanded the hair-dresser, Alice MacQueen.

Priscilla saw them watching her and smiled tentatively. There were no answering smiles, only eyes as hard as Scottish pebbles.

Inside the shop, Hamish was confronting Jock Kennedy, who had been summoned from the back premises by his wife, Ailsa. "Look, Jock," said Hamish, "I know you are running a sort of pub in the back there after hours, and it will chust not do."

Jock scowled ferociously. "Who telt ye?"

"It doesn't matter. You've got to stop it."

"You cannae stop me from having a few friends round."

"No, and I suggest you make it that. If Strathbane heard about it and crashed in here one night, how would things look for me? I am not booking you, Jock, nor am I asking to have a look-see. Chust make sure you're doing nothing illegal in future."

"You should not be bothering an honest man like me," said Jock. "It's that Sassenach you should be after."

"What's he done?"

"He's a dirty fighter. He kicked me in the balls."

Ailsa gave a shrill laugh. "It was self-defence. Hear this, Macbeth. It wass at the ceilidh. Himself here gets thcm to call Peter out fur a dram and as soon as Peter appears, Jock challenges him to a fight. Going to beat him to a pulp, he wass." Ailsa laughed again. "Well, you got your comeuppance, so leave Peter Hynd alone."

"Hiss days here are numbered, wumman."

"I'll leave you both," said Hamish hurriedly. "Don't forget what I said, Jock."

He went outside. He paused for a moment, studying the scene in front of him. Priscilla had turned to face the loch, trying to look unconcerned. The women of Drim had edged closer to her, as if inspecting some rare wild beast.

"Shoo!" said Hamish, running up to them and waving his hands.

Hamish returned to Priscilla, his face grim. "That great fool, Jock Kennedy, challenged Peter Hynd to a fight and Peter kicked him where it hurts the most."

"That's bad," said Priscilla. "A Highlander won't ever forget or forgive that until he gets revenge."

"They'll gang up on him one dark night," said Hamish. "Let's go and see the minister."

"Why?"

"He's supposed to be looking after the morals of his flock."

They went up to the manse and this time Hamish found Mr. Callum Duncan at home as well as his wife, Annie.

They were served tea in the manse living-room, the minister and Hamish exchanging general chit-chat until Annie brought in tea and scones. Hamish noticed that Annie's hair was once more its natural brown colour.

"So what brings you to Drim?" asked the minister at last.

"I'm worried about Peter Hynd."

"Our newcomer?" said the minister. "A most amiable and intelligent young man. Nothing wrong with him, I hope?"

"He's been flirting with the women of your parish." Hamish felt ridiculously like a Victorian reformer. "He's stirring up all sorts of emotions. Have you not noticed the way the women are behaving?"

"Oh, they've been getting a bit silly, but that's women for you," said the minister indulgently. Hamish glanced at Annie Duncan, but her head was bent over the teapot.

"It iss more than that," said Hamish firmly. "There was a fight. Jock Kennedy and Peter Hynd, and Peter . . . er . . . kicked him where he shouldn't have."

"As he was up against an ox like Jock, then I suppose he had to protect himself anyway he could," said Mr. Duncan. "It will all settle down. You know what the Highlands are like. There is always a certain antipathy to the newcomer."

"It is because of this silly antipathy that a lot of good people go away from the Highlands and leave the trash behind," said Hamish bitterly.

Annie's voice came, cool and amused. "Peter Hynd does seem capable of rousing jealousy in men and women alike."

"I am not jealous of the man," said

Hamish. "This is a serious matter. If that young man does not settle down and stop playing silly games with the locals, then someone will stab him. I am taking this verra seriously. Talk to them on the sabbath, minister, and warn them against bitterness, envy, and lust."

"Dear me, and they call poor Callum a Holy Roller," said Annie, sounding amused.

"May I point out that the thing that causes most passions to run high," said the minister, "is strong drink, and we have none of that in Drim."

"Havers," said Hamish. "Every man has his bottle. The fact that it isn't sold openly doesn't stop them drinking, and I'm willing to bet that there's more than one illegal still up in the hills."

"I am sure your motives are of the best." Mr. Duncan's voice was suddenly steely. "You do your job and I will do mine. I am not lax in reminding my flock on Sunday of the virtues of life. Now, may we talk of something more pleasant? Miss Halburton-Smythe, I believe your family home is now a hotel? Does that disturb you, or have you come to accept it?"

Priscilla talked easily of the difficulties of settling into a hotel life while Hamish sat and brooded. Was he perhaps jealous of

Peter Hynd? But he had been uneasy about the man before Peter had ever taken Priscilla out for dinner.

When they emerged from the manse, wreaths of mist were stealing down the sides of the mountains, like long, searching fingers.

At the Land Rover, Priscilla hesitated beside it. "Hamish," she said, "when I went to the seer looking for you, he said an odd thing."

"Aye, what was that?"

"He said a beautiful young man would come between us."

Hamish looked bleakly at the descending mist. "You neffer believed a word that man said before."

"And why should I now?" rejoined Priscilla lightly. "You're quite right, Hamish. This place is enough to give anyone the creeps."

They climbed into the Rover. Hamish released the handbrake. He saw a little figure moving towards them up the road through the mist. Heather Baxter. Her eyes were blank but tears were streaming down her cheeks. He swore under his breath and jerked the brake on again and climbed down. The girl saw him coming and swerved away off the road and began to run across the peatbog beside the loch, off into the mist. "Heather!" called Hamish sharply. "Heather!" But only silence came back to him.

"Something must be wrong at the Baxters'," he said when he rejoined Priscilla. "I'm going over there."

But when they got to the Baxters' cottage, it was closed and silent. No smoke rose from the chimney. Hamish wondered whether to go back into the village and look for Betty Baxter. As he was standing there, irresolute, Heather Baxter came round the side of the cottage. She looked calm and composed. "Oh, Mr. Macbeth," she said. "Can I help you?"

"I saw you crying," said Hamish.

"Me? Och, no, it must haff been a trick o' the mist."

"Where's your ma?"

"Edie Aubrey is running the bingo. She's there."

"Not the exercise class?"

"After it, she sometimes has the bingo."

"And your faither?"

"Up in bed."

"Look, Heather, if there is anything you ever want to talk to me about, phone me up." Hamish scribbled the Lochdubh police-station telephone number on a piece of paper and handed it over.

"Thank you," said Heather, taking the paper, but Hamish noticed she crumpled it up in her hand.

He returned to Priscilla and drove off. Up the twisting road they went, crawling through the now-thick mist until, at the top, they moved out into brilliant sunshine and blue sky. Hamish stopped and looked back. Below them, shrouded somewhere in the mist and at the foot of those black mountains, lay Drim. He shivered.

"I've done my best," he said to Priscilla. "That place gives me weird fancies. Best leave it alone."

And indeed, among the bright heather and with the warmth of the sun striking through the glass, he could feel all his fears melting away. There were a lot of strange places in the Highlands of Scotland where the very earth gave out a bleak atmosphere of misery, as if years of hardship had been recorded in the ancient rock and thin poor soil. They made things seem exaggerated. With a feeling of relief, he drove home to Lochdubh.

That night at two in the morning Peter Hynd was awakened by a sound of breaking glass. He struggled out of bed and climbed down the ladder from his bedroom under the roof. He went into the kitchen and switched on the light. A brick with a piece of paper wrapped round it was lying below the shattered kitchen window. He un-wrapped the paper and smoothed it out on the table. In capital letters was the message: GET OUT OF DRIM OR WE'LL KILL YOU. Betty Baxter descended the ladder from the bedroom with Peter's dressing-gown wrapped around her. "Whit's happened?" she asked.

He showed her the message. "Maybe you'd best go home," he said.

"Harry's out with the fishing and won't be back until the morn," she said. "It's probably Jock and the others. You'd better put something on," she added, looking at Peter's naked body.

"Why? I'm going back to bed. You don't think I'm going to let any of that lot spoil my sleep."

"I'm frightened," whispered Betty.

He pulled her against him and kissed her lips, and neither saw the blur of a face which peered for a moment in from the mist and then disappeared.

Life picked up for Hamish Macbeth in the following weeks, so that he almost forgot about Drim. There had been a series of burglaries over in Carrask, a small village forty miles away but still on his beat. To his distress, his suspicions began to focus on a newcomer, even though Hamish thought most newcomers suffered from undeserved bad reputations. But in this case he believed the culprit was one Sammy Dolan, an itinerant Irish worker who was, at that moment in time, out of work and drawing the dole. He was beginning to despair of getting any hard proof when one of the locals told him that Dolan had been seen earlier in the day prowling around Miss Tabbet's. Miss Tabbet was the local schoolteacher who lived in a neat bungalow outside the village and whose home had so far appeared burglar-proof.

Hamish visited her and suggested he spend the night in her front-room. Miss Tabbet was one of those no-nonsense, brisk women who, despite excellent academic qualifications, was quite stupid.

"Nonsense, Mr. Macbeth," she said. "Any burglar would have more sense than to come here."

Hamish stifled a sigh. Why did he always have to be patient and restrained? He felt like taking hold of her by her scrawny neck and shaking her. He said aloud, "Well, I'll type out a letter which says that I was sure

Dolan would break into your premises this night and you refused our help. I'll do two copies, one for headquarters at Strathbane and one for your insurance company . . ."

"No need for that," she said, looking alarmed. "I'm sure I've done all I could to help the police when the occasion arose."

"This is the occasion."

"Oh, well," she said ungraciously, "you can wait in the living-room, but make sure you wipe your feet. I've just shampooed that carpet. But don't expect me to make cups of tea for you. I pay my taxes and that should be enough. You're wasting your time. This house is burglar-proof."

"How?"

"Come here," she said, and Hamish thought for a moment that she was going to take hold of him by the ear and lead him by it like a bad child. She led the way to the front door and pointed triumphantly to an array of bolts, chains, and safety locks.

"What about the back door?" asked Hamish.

She snorted and led the way through to the kitchen. The back door was similarly armed. Hamish stood back and looked at the kitchen window and a smile crossed his face. "All the man need do is smash a pane in your kitchen window, put an arm in an open the catch."

"But I'd hear the breaking glass," she said triumphantly. "I'm a very light sleeper."

"I could break thon glass without you hearing a thing," said Hamish. "Chust bear with me. I'll be here at six o'clock."

"Why so early?" she jeered. She was a very jeering sort of woman, made so by years of controlling pupils by sarcasm. "Is he coming for his tea?"

"I want to get in here early, before he starts watching the house," said Hamish. He smiled down warmly into her eyes, and despite herself she smiled back and looked up at him in a dazed way.

"You silly man," Hamish chided himself as he walked back down through the village. "You're getting as bad as Peter Hynd." And with that thought, he once more had a mental picture of the dark village of Drim with all those passions seething and bubbling at the end of the loch. He was so preoccupied with his thoughts that he almost walked past Sophy Bisset, who hailed him enthusiastically. "What are you doing here?" asked Hamish in surprise.

"It's my day off and I'm playing tourist," said Sophy. "What are *you* doing here?" She asked, just as if she had never overheard Priscilla telling Mr. Johnston that Hamish was investigating crime in Carrask.

"On duty," said Hamish.

"Time for a cup of tea? There's a place in the back of the craft shop at the end of the village."

"Aye, that'll be grand," said Hamish. He felt a warm glow. He did not for a moment believe that Sophy had not known he was to be found in Carrask, and that meant she had come in search of him whereas Priscilla had not; Priscilla who, before their engagement, would have dropped over to see him. That Priscilla was badly frightened by any intimacy was becoming clearer and clearer, and Hamish was beginning to think that his hopes that it would "be all right on the night," namely on their honeymoon, were beginning to look naïve in the extreme. Meanwhile, here was pretty Sophy with her sparkling eyes appearing delighted with his company. And a friendly bird in Carrask was worth two chilly ones in Lochdubh any day. He was hurt and angry with Priscilla and it was with a feeling of revenge that he set out to be especially charming to Sophy in the pepper-scented back room of the craft shop.

At last he looked at his watch. "I must be on my way," he said with genuine regret. They walked out together. "See you back in

Lochdubh, then," said Sophy. She stood on tiptoe and kissed him on the cheek.

Across the street Mrs. Fair, who owned the small hotel called Carrask Arms, watched curiously and then she picked up the phone. "Is that the Tommel Castle Hotel?" she asked. "Good. May I speak to Miss Halburton-Smythe?"

Hamish was glad of the tea and cakes he had shared with Sophy in the afternoon as the long evening wore on. He would have liked to watch television to pass the time but Miss Tabbet had recovered from the glow that smile of his had given her and said she "didn't hold with it," and Hamish wondered crossly why she had the thing in the first place. She sat and knitted fiercely while listening to a concert on the radio, a modern piece by a Hungarian composer full of crashing minor chords. At last, to Hamish's relief, she went up to bed. He was amused to hear loud snores reverberating through the ceiling a short time later. Miss Tabbet slept like a pig, he thought. A whole gang of burglars could crash in without her hearing anything.

He looked at the clock. It was only ten. He switched on the television set and watched the news and then a programme in

Gaelic, inevitably about the history of the Highland Clearances, when the crofters were driven off their land. Then a very fat Glaswegian woman sang a dirge about the clearances she had written herself, and apart from being briefly fascinated to hear Gaelic sung with all the glottal stops of a Glaswegian accent, Hamish became bored and switched it off.

The minutes dragged on. At midnight, he switched off the downstairs lights and sat in the darkness. The nights were getting darker and he knew that by two o'clock there would be about one hour of guaranteed darkness and that, he guessed, would be when Dolan struck, if it was Dolan who had been guilty of the other break-ins.

Two o'clock came and went and he yawned and stretched. Nothing was going to happen, he decided. Miss Tabbet was an old battleaxe and even Dolan must have decided to give her house a miss. The wind had risen and was howling outside. But suddenly he heard it. The tinkle of breaking glass coming from the kitchen.

He went quietly to the back of the house. A hand crept through a hole in the glass of the kitchen window and released the catch. Then the burly figure of a man climbed in over the draining-board and jumped lightly onto the floor.

Hamish switched on the kitchen light.

Sammy Dolan stood there, blinking at him. But before Hamish could charge him, Dolan whipped a wicked hunting-knife out of his boot.

"Stand back," he said, "and no one will get hurt."

Hamish reached behind him, picked up a frying pan from the cooker and then, darting forward like lightning and ducking to avoid a vicious stab of the knife, brought it down with all his force on Dolan's forehead.

The Irishman groaned and fell to the kitchen floor. He was down but not out, so Hamish dragged him across the floor and handcuffed him to the iron leg of the cooker, read out the charge and then went through and called Strathbane and asked them to send help to pick Dolan up.

He returned to the kitchen. Dolan looked up at him balefully and let out a stream of oaths. "Shut up," said Hamish. He went upstairs in the direction of the snores. Miss Tabbet was lying on her back, her face glistening with cold cream. He put a hand on her shoulder and shook her awake.

"Get out of my bedroom, you . . . you *rapist*," she screamed.

"The day I even think about raping someone like you I'll check into the loony-bin," said Hamish brutally. "I've caught your burglar."

"What?" Miss Tabbet was obviously reluctant to let the thought of rape disappear.

"I've caught the burglar. I'm waiting for the van from Strathbane to take him away."

She struggled up. "Where is he?"

"Handcuffed to your kitchen cooker." Hamish turned and walked out and went back down to the kitchen.

Dolan was quieter, but at the sight of Hamish he said, "I'm going to charge you with police brutality."

"Suit yourself," Hamish shrugged and went to plug in the kettle. He felt he deserved·a coffee.

Miss Tabbet appeared in the doorway wrapped in a pink chenille dressing-gown and stared at the figure of Dolan on the floor. Then her eyes went to the frying-pan, which Hamish had tossed onto the counter. She picked it up. "Why has my best frying-pan got a dunt in it?"

"Because I hit Dolan on the head with it."

"Police brutality, that's what it is," whined Dolan.

"My best frying-pan," screeched Miss Tabbet. "And what are you doing with that kettle?"

"You can put in a bill for the frying-pan if you like," said Hamish coolly. "And as I have chust saved you from being robbed, you can allow me one cup of coffee." His voice was quiet, but something in it made Miss Tabbet blink rapidly and retreat. To Hamish's relief, he heard her going back upstairs. He made himself a cup of instant coffee and took it through to the living-room and waited patiently until a police van arrived from Strathbane and took Dolan away. It was six in the morning. He should really wake the schoolteacher again and ask her to lock up after he went but he could not bear any more of her grumbling, and besides, the burglar had been caught. He took a childish delight in leaving his un-washed coffee-cup on the living-room table. He went out into the light of a sunny morning, climbed into the Land Rover, and with a feeling of gladness, of release, set off for Lochdubh.

After filing his report he slept most of the day and then awoke and phoned Priscilla. Sophy answered the phone and said she would find her. After quite a long time she came back and said in an amused voice that Priscilla had said she was out. "And what's she miffed about?" asked Hamish.

114

"Some biddy reported we were seen kissing outside the craft shop in Carrask," said Sophy gleefully.

"I hope you told Priscilla there was nothing in that," said Hamish sharply.

"Oh, sure. But she wasn't inclined to listen to me."

"I'll be right up." Hamish slammed down the phone, cursing Sophy under his breath.

He could feel his engagement, unofficial though it still was, falling apart. He no longer knew what he wanted. Why had Priscilla turned into such a managing female? Why couldn't she have left him alone? He suddenly wondered if she would ever change. Would she clatter around the police station in Lochdubh eternally unforgiving when she finally realized he had no intention of leaving the village? Why couldn't people realize it was a rare gift to be happy with one's lot? Although this particular policeman's lot at the present moment, and thanks to Priscilla and Sophy, was not a happy one.

When he got to the hotel, Sophy said happily she would fetch Priscilla while Hamish paced up and down the reception. When Priscilla and Sophy walked in, Sophy went back behind the reception desk and leaned on it.

"Yes, Hamish?" asked Priscilla frostily.

He gathered her in his arms and she suddenly gave a little sigh and leaned against him. Sophy watched wide-eyed as Hamish, with his arm about Priscilla's shoulders, led her outside.

"Now what's all this?" asked Hamish gently.

"I couldn't help remembering your reputation as a philanderer," said Priscilla in a low voice.

"Look, you must know that Sophy found out that I was at Carrask and followed me over. We went for tea and then she kissed my cheek on leaving. That was all. But I couldnae help remembering the days when you yourself would have come over to see me."

"I've been pretty bad, haven't I, Hamish? Forget about promotion and houses in Strathbane. I'm sure we'll be happy enough in the Lochdubh police station."

"Come back with me now," urged Hamish. "We never have any proper time together."

For one awful moment, she hesitated and then she nodded her fair head.

Hamish's excitement rose as he approached the police station, with Priscilla following in her own car. This was it, at last!

116

Were there clean sheets on the bed? Damn, he needed a bath. He hadn't had any supper and his stomach grumbled and rumbled. But food could wait.

Once inside the police station, he brushed aside Priscilla's suggestion that they should have a cup of coffee and gathered her firmly in his arms. The time had come for action. He swept her up to carry her to the bedroom but she was a tall girl and her feet got jammed in the kitchen door.

"Put me down," laughed Priscilla. "I can walk."

Hamish put her down and just as he did so, the bell at the front police-station door rang shrilly and urgently.

They both looked at each other. The locals all used the back door. Only strangers rang the bell at the front.

"It'll only take a minute," said Hamish breathlessly. "Probably one o' thae tourists lost something up on the moors."

The wind was buffeting the police station and the blue lamp outside was swinging wildly as he opened the door. He dropped his gaze.

The small figure of Heather Baxter stood on the doorstep.

In her lilting Highland accent, she said, "I haff come to report a murder."

CHAPTER 5

No, no, he is dead;
Go to thy death-bed,
He will never come again.

William Shakespeare

"Come in," said Hamish quietly. He took
Heather's cold, damp hand and led her
through to the kitchen. "Hot, sweet tea," he
said to Priscilla.

He pushed Heather into a chair and
crouched down in front of her. "Who's been
murdered?"

"Thon Sassenach, Peter Hynd."

"How wass he killed?"

She shook her head dumbly.

"Where wass the body found?"

"It has not been found."

Hamish straightened up and sat down
next to her. "Then how do you know he has
been murdered?"

She looked at him with those odd grey eyes and then she pointed to her head. "I saw it in here," she whispered. "They all say he's gone. He left a note. His things are gone. But I know he's been murdered. I *feel* him around the village."

Hamish took a mug of tea from Priscilla and handed it to Heather. "Drink this," he urged. "How did you get here?"

"I drove in my faither's truck. I tied blocks on my feet and drove. He's drunk asleep. He did not go to the fishing."

"You've had a hard time at home recently, Heather," said Hamish, "and maybe that's what's been putting these thoughts in your head." She shook that head stubbornly. "This is what we'll do. I won't be booking you for driving without a licence. That will be our secret. But neffer do such a thing again. Then I will drive you back in the truck and Priscilla here will follow us. She'll bring me back and then I'll return in the morning and start asking questions."

Heather looked up at Priscilla and a strangely feminine look for one of her tender years crossed her face. Her grey eyes slanted at Hamish. "I don't want her."

"Then how am I to get back?"

"I'll drive myself," said Heather. "I've already broken the law driving here. One more time won't matter."

Hamish sighed. "I'd better get her back, Priscilla."

"That's all right, Hamish," said Priscilla, making for the door. "See you tomorrow."

"I won't be long," said Hamish defiantly. "Won't you wait?"

"Tomorrow," said Priscilla firmly.

Hamish felt a sudden flash of murderous anger. She was going to be a policeman's wife. This was a fine start! But he waited patiently until Heather had finished her tea. "Where's the truck?" he asked.

"It is outside at the side of the station."

"Come along then. I'll follow you."

She went outside and Hamish waited while she put on a man's overcoat and cap and then strapped wooden blocks onto her feet so that she could reach the pedals. He waited until she had reversed out into the road, climbed into the Land Rover and followed her. In his lights, with her cap pulled down, she looked like a man. To his relief she drove quickly and competently over the roads and down into Drim. She parked outside, untied the blocks from her feet and climbed down from the truck. "They sleep like the dead," she whispered. "I'll creep in. Don't tell anyone. Chust come tomorrow."

Hamish nodded and waited. She opened

the house door gently and slipped inside.

He drove off, his thoughts grim. He hoped to God that Heather was mistaken, that Peter Hynd had simply taken himself off.

A sunny morning restored his spirits and banished most of the ghosts of the night before, although he was still furious with Priscilla.

He went straight to the general stores in Drim. "I heard that Peter Hynd had left," he said to Jock Kennedy. "When was that?"

"Two weeks ago," said Jock. "Found a note from him pushed in the shop letter-box along with the key. Said he'd gone off south and left the sale of the cottage in the hands o' Cummings and Bane, the estate agents in Strathbane."

"Still got the note?"

"Yes, I hae it here." He ferreted around under the counter and came up with a folded piece of paper. Hamish opened it and read it. It was type-written and unsigned. "Got bored," it said, "and am putting the cottage up for sale. Could you give the key to any prospective buyer, Jock? The agents are Cummings and Bane, Strathbane. My solicitors are Brand and MacDougal, Castle Wynd, Inverness. Peter Hynd." But the "Peter Hynd" was type-written.

Hamish frowned down at the letter. "Any takers?" he said at last.

"Aye, there was a big fellow, a builder from Newcastle, up the other day. Hynd's only asking fifteen thousand."

"I doubt if he'll get that. Did he finish the drainage?"

"No."

"Well . . ."

"But the field at the back goes wi' the house. This chap from Newcastle, he wass talking about maybe getting building permission. Wants it for a holiday cottage." And with a fine disregard for any European Market directives on hygiene, Jock spat contemptuously on the shop floor.

"I've no doubt you'll give him a right Highland welcome," said Hamish drily. "Let me have the key, Jock. I'll take a look around."

For one brief moment Hamish thought he was going to refuse, but after a short hesitation the big man took down a key from a nail behind the counter and handed it over.

Hamish left the Land Rover where it was and walked up to Peter's cottage. He let himself in and stood sniffing the air. Towser, who had followed him in, sniffed the air as well. "Nobody been in here for a while," said Hamish. "Let's look about."

Peter had left the pots and pans and dishes behind but the camping stove had gone. There were half-empty packets of grocery goods in the cupboards. A small fridge was switched off and proved empty. At the back of the house were piles of wood and bricks, showing that Peter had meant to start on the extension. Tools were lying on the floor and a couple of trestles held planks waiting to be sawn. Hamish shook his head. Surely Peter would have wanted to finish the work and, therefore, get a better price. There were also piles of slates showing where he had meant to take off the iron roof and replace it with a proper one.

Hamish went through to the parlour, which Peter had used as a dining-room-cum-sitting-room. There was nothing of value left, no television, no radio, and no books, just some pieces of furniture. Hamish went back to the living-room, which Peter had used as a kitchen. He picked up the ladder lying against the wall and climbed up to the trapdoor in the ceiling, and pushed it open and climbed through. He found himself in the bedroom. There was a low double bed against one wall, with a low table beside it. There were no sheets or blankets on the bed. He searched around the corners of the room, but all he could find was one hairpin. He held it up to the light coming through the skylight. It was a blonde-coloured pin. He put it in his pocket and climbed down the stairs again.

He scratched his head. Why would Peter leave a note with Jock Kennedy, of all people? He locked up and put the key in his pocket.

As he strolled back down, he could hear the beat of music coming from the community hall. He went up to it and pushed open the door. Only four women were gyrating to the music. He waited patiently until the tape finished and then approached Edie Aubrey. She pushed back her lank hair and blinked at him through her thick glasses.

"Not many women," commented Hamish.

"No," agreed Edie sadly, "things are not the same."

"Since Hynd left?"

"Why did he go just like that?" muttered Edie. She picked a towel up from a chair and wiped her forehead. "He might at least have called to say goodbye."

"Did anyone see him go?" asked Hamish.

"Nobody's really spoken to me about it." Hamish turned and surveyed the women. Nancy Macleod was there, grey roots now showing in the black dye of her hair. She looked much smaller and older. Ailsa, Jock's wife, was sipping coffee and talking to Betty Baxter. The other woman he did not know. They were all suddenly older, thought Hamish, as if the life had gone out of them. He approached Betty Baxter. "Is Harry at home?"

"Aye, the silly fool got drunk and couldnae go to the fishing."

"I'll maybe drop by for a word."

"Why?" asked Betty sharply.

"I'm trying to find out why Peter Hynd left, or if anyone saw him leave."

"And what's that got to do with Harry?"

"He may have heard or seen something, that's all."

"There's no crime," said Betty with a shrill laugh. "For heffen's sake, the man's gone, put his house up for sale, and that's that."

"Nevertheless, I'll be having a word with Harry." Hamish touched his cap and left.

Harry Baxter was sitting at the kitchen table, staring at nothing in particular.

"Rough night?" asked Hamish sympathetically.

Harry stared at him moodily but did not reply.

"Any reason why Hynd left?" pursued Hamish.

Harry made an obvious effort to gather his wits together. "Och, he wass jist playing himself at being a Highlander. Gone back south, I believe."

"Did anyone see him go?"

"Folks reckon he left during the night."

"Any trouble with the villagers before he left?"

"Why should there be?"

"Don't be daft," said Hamish crossly. "All you men hated him and with good reason."

"He's jist gone, that's all. Haven't ye mair to do than look for a murder that doesn't exist?"

"I didn't say anything about murder. Where's Heather?"

"At school. School's started."

"Keep an eye on that lassie o' yours, Harry. I think those rows you've been having with Betty are upsetting her."

"Mind your ain business," snapped Harry.

Hamish decided to try Jimmy Macleod but when he went out to the Land Rover, his radio crackled into life. He looked at it in mild surprise. He hardly ever got a call on it. It was Detective Jimmy Anderson, asking him to report immediately to Strathbane, to the chief superintendent's office.

Hamish's gloomy thought was that his boss had finally got into the act and that promotion and Strathbane were an inevitability. He had a shrewd idea that hitherto the chief superintendent had kept apart from his wife's ambitious plans.

But whatever had happened to Peter Hynd would have to wait for another day.

As he walked into police headquarters he was met by his bête noire, Detective Chief Inspector Blair. Blair's fat features creased into a smile. "On yer way upstairs," he said. "My, my. Have fun."

Hamish frowned. If Blair had got wind of any possible promotion for Hamish Macbeth, he would have been in a foul mood. With a sinking feeling he took the lift up to the sixth floor. The chief superintendent's secretary, Helen Jessop, was typing efficiently. She looked up when he entered. "You'll need to wait," she said, "he's busy," and went on typing.

"Any idea what it's about?" asked Hamish.

"You'll just need to find out," said Helen, ripping out one sheet and screwing in another.

"Why don't you have a word processor instead of that old-fashioned thing?" asked Hamish.

"This machine has served me very well. I don't hold with computers," said Helen.

"Meaning you don't know anything about

them and are too frightened to find out," said Hamish maliciously. "It's known as technofear. The plague of the middle-aged."

Helen snorted by way of reply.

"Any chance of a cup of tea?" asked Hamish.

"No."

Hamish sat and fidgeted. He could hear the hum of voices from inside Peter Daviot's office. The shelf behind Helen's desk was a jungle of depressing greenhouse plants. Secretaries with house-plants were a threatening breed, thought Hamish. As time dragged by, he grew more uneasy. It was like waiting outside the headmaster's office. At last the door opened and five men in business suits came out.

"I am about to interview the officer in question," said Mr. Daviot, "and I will give you my full report."

The suits turned as one man and looked Hamish up and down before filing out. One of the men's voices floated back to Hamish's sharp ears. "Doesn't look violent, but you never can tell."

"Come in, Macbeth," said Mr. Daviot. No "Hamish." A warning sign like a stormcone hoisted over Hamish's head. He tucked his cap under his arm and stood meekly in front of the super's desk.

"Sit down," said Mr. Daviot. "Sorry to keep you waiting. Helen been looking after you?"

"She refused to get me a cup of tea," said Hamish, hoping he was sliding the knife into Helen's corseted ribs.

"Come into the twentieth century, Macbeth. You don't go around ordering tea from secretaries or they'll report you to the Equal Opportunities Board or something."

"Why, sir?"

"Making and fetching tea is demeaning."

"I don't get it," said Hamish puzzled. "Isn't it the same as 'Type this letter,' 'Make this phone call,' 'Order flowers for my wife'?"

"It implies you are treating a business woman like a housewife."

"I don't get it. A housewife can say, 'Get the damn thing yourself.' A secretary can't."

"Because . . . Look, I did not bring you here to talk about Women's Lib. There has been a serious charge laid against you."

"By whom?"

"By Sammy Dolan."

"That toe-rag! What's he saying?"

"He's filed a complaint of police brutality. He's got a lawyer. He says you hit him with a frying-pan and he's got a lump on his head to prove it."

"I hit him with the frying-pan because he was resisting arrest, or, to put it more bluntly, had I not hit him, he would have knifed me. I filed a full report."

"Just tell me again, in your own words."

Hamish felt a stab of irritation. He suddenly wanted to say, "No, I'll tell you in someone else's words," and imitate Blair's thick Glasgow accent and boorish manner.

"I had reason to believe that Dolan meant to break into the schoolteacher's house," he said patiently. "Just after two in the morning, I heard the sound of breaking glass in the kitchen and went through. Dolan had smashed the glass. He opened the catch and climbed into the kitchen. I switched on the light. He took a hunting-knife out of his boot and came at me. I reached behind me and picked up the frying-pan. Before he could knife me, I hit him on the head. He fell to the floor, stunned but still conscious. I handcuffed him to the cooker. I read the charge, phoned Strathbane, and waited until the van arrived. That's all."

"Miss Tabbet, who is claiming for a new frying-pan, says you had an insolent manner. You approached her in her bedroom, you made yourself coffee without her permission, and you went off leaving everything unlocked and your dirty cup on the living-room table. She, too, has lodged a complaint."

Hamish could feel himself already being enmeshed in a nightmarish web of red tape. He carefully explained in detail what had happened when he had awoken the schoolteacher and why he had gone without waking her again.

Mr. Daviot sighed. "You make it all sound very reasonable and I must admit that Miss Tabbet is a tiresome female. But to return to Dolan. We are very anxious to avoid charges of brutality. Think what the press will make of this."

"I'll bet you Dolan's got previous," said Hamish.

"Well, he has. Quite a lot."

"Grievous bodily harm, actual bodily harm, that sort of thing?"

"Yes, and armed robbery."

"Well, there you —"

"Macbeth, you have always had an unorthodox way of going about things. The sensible course, the minute you suspected Dolan was going to break into that house, would have been to have ordered back-up from Strathbane. Two of you could have overpowered the man without resorting to violence."

"There's little even several men can do

131

against a hunting-knife in the hands of a man like Dolan without using violence."

"My other officers don't get themselves into situations like this," said Mr. Daviot, with a trace of pettishness creeping into his voice.

"I made an arrest, sir. I stopped the burglaries. And instead of getting thanks, all I get is carpeted because a dangerous criminal takes it into his thick head to have a go at me."

"We're all very grateful to you. But this complaint has been made and you will need to go before the inquiry board. I suggest you curb that insolent manner of yours, Macbeth. Now, are you engaged in anything else at the moment?"

"Just one little thing. There was a newcomer over at Drim, an Englishman. He left the village but no one saw him go. He left a note to say his house was on the market."

"So?"

"He had caused a lot of trouble in the village by flirting with the women. The men hated him. There's something about it all I don't like."

"If he has put his house on the market, it seems to me as if he is very much all right. Did he leave everything behind?"

"No."

"There you are. I know crime has been thin on the ground on your patch, but there is no need to go around inventing any. I want you to go downstairs and find a desk and type up a full report on the arrest of Dolan for me."

"Very good, sir."

Hamish went out. Helen was not there but there was a full cup of hot tea on her desk. He picked it up and took it with him. He went in search of Jimmy Anderson and found him in the canteen.

"You're in favour," said Jimmy.

"Makes a nice change," rejoined Hamish.

"Aye, it's not often the steely Helen lets anyone have a cup of tea, let alone in her favourite cup."

Startled, Hamish looked at the cup in his hand, which was decorated with roses. He had a sudden feeling that taking Helen's teacup was going to land him in worse disgrace than anything Dolan could throw at him. "Back in a moment," he said.

He went straight to Chief Detective Inspector Blair's room and popped his head round the door. It was empty. He darted in and put Helen's cup on the desk and then returned to the canteen.

He got himself a cup of tea and a plate of egg and chips and rejoined Jimmy.

"So Dolan's got it in for you," said Jimmy. "You know what's odd about that?"

"Apart from damned cheek, no."

"Our beloved leader, Blair, paid a visit on Dolan. Not his case really. All sewn up tidy. Dolan admitted to the other burglaries in Carrask. Quiet as a lamb. So Blair comes out wi' a fat grin on his unlovely face and the next thing Dolan's ringing his bell and calling fur a lawyer and filing a complaint against one Hamish Macbeth."

"That bastard!"

"Aye, well, there you are."

"And where's Dolan now?"

"In the remand wing o' Strathbane pokey awaiting trial."

Hamish gloomily ate his egg and chips and then went down and borrowed Jimmy's desk and filed his second report on the arrest of Dolan. His thoughts turned to Priscilla. He felt alone with his problems and wanted to unburden himself. But before he returned to Lochdubh, he might as well check the estate agent's.

Cummings and Bane was the same estate agent as the one he had visited with Priscilla. This time he told the young man who he was officially and asked about the sale of Peter's house.

"Yes, that's all in order," said the young

man. "Mr. Hynd called on us personally. We think we may have a sale already. We have the name of the lawyers in Inverness."

"I have that," said Hamish moodily. That was that. No mystery.

He drove back to Lochdubh and went straight to Tommel Castle. He had forgotten about his anger at Priscilla but experienced it again when he saw her looking cool and remote. But he needed to unburden himself. He told her first about how his investigations in Drim had been cut short. She listened carefully to his tale of Dolan and Miss Tabbet. When he had finished, she said, "Would you like me to have a word with Susan Daviot?"

"That wouldn't help. There's nothing she can do. Dolan's made the complaint, got a lawyer, and the whole thing will grind on to an inquiry and then I will probably be suspended. I've put up too many backs in Strathbane."

"Nonetheless, I'll see what I can do."

"Och, what the hell can *you* do," snapped Hamish, suddenly disgusted by what he saw as her cool detachment from him.

Priscilla sadly watched him go. It was all such a mess. Why hadn't she waited for him at the police station? But she did not want to answer her own question, so she turned her mind to Hamish's story.

She went through to the office and phoned Susan Daviot. "Hamish is in trouble and all because of this fool Dolan," said Priscilla.

Mrs. Daviot's voice lacked its usual ingratiating warmth. "It seems to me, Priscilla, as if Hamish went over the top. Now Dolan's sister is making trouble and threatening to talk to the newspapers before the inquiry."

"What's her name?"

"Bridget Dolan."

"And where does she live?"

"That's clessified information."

"Dear me, aren't we being a trifle stupid, Susan?" Priscilla was at her haughtiest.

"But I cannot tell you secret information. Never mind. When are we meeting for a little chet?"

"I am going to be *much* too busy in the future, Susan."

Susan Daviot saw her social ambitions biting the dust. "Come to think of it, I did hear that the Dolan woman was living at number forty, Winnie Mandela Court."

"Thank you, Susan. I've just remembered, next Tuesday is a quiet day if you would care to come for tea."

Mrs. Daviot sent up a heartfelt prayer of thanks to the god who looks after social climbers. "*Thenk* you, Priscilla, dear."

Priscilla grinned and put down the phone. She went out and drove off to Carrask and parked in front of the schoolteacher's house and waited patiently while the afternoon wore on. At last she saw a figure who could only be the schoolteacher returning and climbed out of the car. "Miss Tabbet?"

Miss Tabbet swung round and looked favourably at the elegant creature in front of her. "What can I do for you, Miss . . . ?"

"Miss Churchill. I represent the *Daily Bugle.*"

The smile faded on Miss Tabbet's face. The *Daily Bugle* was one of Britain's sleaziest tabloids.

"And what do you want with me?" asked Miss Tabbet.

"You made a report to Strathbane police which contained complaints against a certain police sergeant, Hamish Macbeth. In it, you said he had come into your bedroom."

"Yes, but —"

"Good stuff, that," said Priscilla cheerfully. " 'Schoolmarm lures copper into her bedroom.' "

"But he burst into my room when I was asleep."

" 'The Sexy Copper'? Even better."

"This is dreadful," said Miss Tabbet. "I do not want my name in the papers. I have always been a respectable body. You ruin people. Look what you did to dear Prince Chrles! I will have you stopped."

"As long as you've made an official complaint. Come on. Let's go indoors. My photographer will be along in a minute and I want to be ahead of the pack."

"THE PACK!"

"Yes, they'll all be along. Maybe you'd like to fix your hair and put on a shorter skirt."

"I'm withdrawing any complaint," screamed Miss Tabbet.

"But that means there'll be no story!" cried Priscilla.

"That's it then. I'm doing it now. Get out of my way."

Priscilla watched with amusement as the terrified teacher scampered to a garage at the side of the bungalow. Moments later an old Rover was backed out, with Miss Tabbet crouched over the wheel. She turned and drove off down the road in the direction of Strathbane.

Waiting until she was out of sight, Priscilla followed along the Strathbane road at a leisurely speed.

When she arrived in Strathbane, she took out a folder of maps and selected a street map of Strathbane and located Winnie Mandela Court and drove there. It turned out to be one of those depressing Stalinist tower blocks boasting a broken urine-smelling elevator and acres of graffiti. Priscilla trudged up the stairs. A group of skinheads barred her way on the first landing. "I am from the Social Security Department," said Priscilla frostily, "investigating dole claims."

They shrank back and let her past. Priscilla reflected that if she had said she was a policewoman, they would probably have beaten her up.

Finally she reached number 40 along a rubbish-littered balcony which afforded a view of the grim harbour. The door was answered by a massive woman with dyed-blonde hair and a face so covered with broken veins that it looked like an ordnance-survey map. "What d'ye want?" she asked, the watery eyes of the habitual drinker raking Priscilla up and down.

"I am from the *Daily Bugle*," said Priscilla. "We are interested in buying your brother's story about police brutality."

"Come in," said Bridget eagerly. "I phoned youse lot up but you says you weren't interested."

"Some amateur took the call." Priscilla

was ushered into a living-room which was awful in its filth and dreariness. She sat down on a hard chair after looking suspiciously at the greasy stains on the upholstered ones.

"I'll tell you all I know," said Bridget.

"My newspaper is prepared to pay a large sum, but I need to see your brother in person. Do you by any chance have a visitor's pass?"

Her eyes gleamed. "I have one for tomorrow morning — ten o'clock."

Priscilla opened her handbag and took out her wallet. She extracted two twenties. "Just something on account." Bridget snatched up the notes and tucked them down somewhere near her heavy bosom. She went over to a battered handbag on an equally battered sideboard and took out a pass. "How much will the *Bugle* pay?" she asked. "Thousands?"

"It's up to the editor."

Refusing all invitations of tea, stout, and gin, Priscilla took her leave. She drove off and parked in the multi-storey in the centre and decided to call at the estate agent's, Cummings and Bane, just to see if there were any more properties on the market. She would not nag Hamish into staying in Strathbane, but there might be something between Lochdubh and Strathbane.

The young man leaped up to greet her, as hopeful as ever. He produced folders of houses and Priscilla sat down and went through them. She came to Peter Hynd's cottage and looked at it curiously. She tapped it with her finger-nail. "I knew Mr. Hynd," she said. "Any idea why he left?"

"Och, I don't think I thought to ask," said the young man. "You know how it is, the English come and go. Are you interested, Miss Halburton-Smythe?"

"Not in Drim, no. Exceptionally beautiful young man, Mr. Hynd." Priscilla opened another folder.

"I couldn't say," said the estate agent.

Priscilla looked up quickly. "But you saw him!"

"Aye, but he had such a bad cold, poor man. His voice was rasping and he had a scarf up round his face. He said he was protecting us from his germs."

"What colour of hair?"

"I can't say as I can remember. Tracey, do you call to mind that young Mr. Hynd, the one with the property over in Drim?"

"The one wi' the cold?"

"Aye, him. What colour was his hair?"

"Fairish, I think. Had one of those deer-stalkers on, like Sherlock Holmes."

Priscilla stored up this information to tell Hamish. She looked through some more folders but with the feeling that Hamish Macbeth would not like any of them. She thanked the young man and left. She was reluctant to return to Lochdubh. She decided to buy herself a tooth-brush, a change of clothes, and check into The Highlander, Strathbane's main hotel, and stay the night. It would be pleasant to be in someone else's hotel for a change.

Just before ten in the morning she joined the queue of depressed and depressing women waiting to get into the prison. Some of the women tried to engage her in conversation but she snubbed them, being tired of making up stories about herself and so, to a sort of Greek chorus of "Stuck-up bitch," she finally made her way into the prison.

Dolan appeared on the other side of the glass and stared at the vision that was Priscilla in amazement.

"They said it was my sister," he exclaimed.

"Listen very hard to me," said Priscilla, leaning forward. "I am Hamish Macbeth's fiancée, and I am here to tell you that if you do not withdraw your complaint of police brutality, I will have a word with the sheriff, who is a personal friend, and make sure you are put away for a long stretch in Inverness prison, where Hamish has many friends among the warders. Not only that, I have many connections and I will hound you, both inside prison or out, even if it means sending one of the gamekeepers after you with a gun."

"Wait till I tell the polis about you," jeered Dolan. "More threats."

"And who will they believe?" she mocked. "Me or you? Go ahead. I will prove you are a liar. I'm out for your blood, Dolan."

Dolan looked at her beautiful and implacable face and cringed. He believed every word she said. Like quite a lot of criminals, he thought he was often in prison because society was unfair, because "They" had had it in for him since the day of his birth, "They" being the establishment. He was sure this beautiful bitch would poison the sheriff's mind.

"And if I withdraw the complaint, will ye have a word in my favour with the sheriff?" said Dolan.

"Of course."

"Oh, well, I suppose," he grumbled.

"Do it," hissed Priscilla.

Later that day, a surprised Hamish Macbeth received a call from Jimmy Anderson to tell him that not only had Miss Tabbet withdrawn her complaint against him — not to mention her claim for a new frying-pan — but that Dolan had withdrawn his complaint as well.

"Thank heavens," said Hamish. "I wonder what came over them."

"Aye, it's the grand day for you, Hamish, because when Dolan was pressed to say why he had made the complaint in the first place, he said Blair had talked him into it. So Blair's on the carpet."

Hamish decided to drive up to Tommel Castle and tell Priscilla about it and found her just arriving as he drove up.

After he had told her his news, he listened in amazement as she told him her part in it and then said in admiration, "Ye get more like me every day."

"Yes, I'm turning out to be a good liar," agreed Priscilla. "I'll be poaching my father's salmon next. But there's something else." She told him about the mysterious Peter Hynd who had appeared at the estate agent's muffled up to the eyebrows.

His hazel eyes gleamed. "I'd better get down to Inverness and see those lawyers. What was the name again? Ah, Brand and MacDougal in Castle Wynd. I'll drive down tomorrow." They had walked into the hotel reception as they were speaking. "Would you care to come with me?"

"I'd love to, but there's a new party of guests arriving tomorrow."

"I'll let you know how I get on. Free for dinner tonight?"

Her face took on a guarded look. "I've got to check the accounts with Mr. Johnston, but if I get through it quickly enough, I'll drive down and see you."

He masked his disappointment and irritation with an effort. She had done sterling work in getting him off the hook with those complaints, and he fought down a feeling that he would gladly have faced any inquiry board in return for a warmer and less efficient fiancée.

Sophy's cheek swelled up alarmingly that day. By evening she was complaining loudly about the pain and Priscilla reluctantly agreed that Sophy should have the following day off to visit the dentist.

So a happy Sophy drove off in the direction of Inverness in the morning, only stopping to take the lump of candle wax out of her cheek and toss it into the heather.

CHAPTER 6

He gave way to the queer, savage feeling that sometimes takes by the throat a husband twenty years' married, when he sees, across the table, the same face of his wedded wife, and knows that, as he has sat facing it, so must he continue to sit until the day of its death or his own.

Rudyard Kipling

Hamish arrived in Inverness in a sour mood. Priscilla had failed to turn up the previous evening and he had been too proud to phone her. "A fine friend she is," he muttered to himself, forgetting that friends are one thing and people with whom one is emotionally involved quite something else. He would simply have phoned a friend and said, "Where the hell are you?"

An autumn chill was making the smoky Inverness air feel raw. He parked at the station and walked round to the Castle Wynd.

Inverness as usual was packed with shoppers. Britain might be lurching along the bottom of a deep recession, but there was little evidence of it in Inverness. Sea-gulls wheeled overhead as shoppers crammed the pavements.

He found the lawyers' brass plate and went up an old staircase of shallow stone stairs flanked by an iron-and-wood banister with brass spikes on the top, no doubt to stop happy clients from sliding down them.

He went into the hush of a Victorian office. Gloomy light filtered through the grimy windows. A tired-looking girl sat at a large wooden desk doing something with her nails.

"Police," said Hamish. "I want to see one of the lawyers."

She rose and went to an oak door, rapped on it, and put her head around it. "Polis to see you, Mr. Brand." There was a mumbled answer and she jerked her head at Hamish. "You're to go in."

Hamish reflected that it was the lawyers, not the police, who were getting younger these days. Mr. Brand was a slight young man with thick wavy hair and an ingenuous face. He was holding a collie pup on his lap when Hamish entered. He rose and put the dog in a basket in the corner of the room.

"Great little fellow," he said. "Very good for the battered wives. Puts them at ease. Now how can I help you, Sergeant?"

Hamish explained about Peter Hynd and asked if he had signed the papers. "Yes, a delightful man. I gather from the estate agents that they might have a buyer already. Odd, that, with castles and mansions going for a song these days, and then a run-down croft house with unfinished drains comes on the market and it's snapped up."

"What did he look like?" asked Hamish.

"Good-looking fellow. Fair. English. Upper class. Why all the questions?"

"I just wondered if it might have been someone impersonating him," said Hamish, although, from the description, he wondered who on earth it could be. Neither Jock Kennedy nor Harry Baxter, say, could have been labelled either fair, English, or upper class by any stretch of the imagination.

"I shouldn't think so. I mean, when the money comes through, it's to be paid into his bank in London. The City and London Bank in New Bond Street. What makes you think someone might have been impersonating him?"

"He had caused a lot of ill feeling in the village of Drim and then he disappeared, and no one seems to have seen him go. He left a note with Jock Kennedy at the general store and he had been involved in a fight with Kennedy. The minister would have been a more believable choice. But if, as you say, he signed the papers . . ."

"Well, we can easily check that. I'll fax his signature to his bank and ask for confirmation."

Hamish, looking around the dusty, gloomy old-fashioned office, was amazed that it contained such a modern item as a fax machine, but Mr. Brand went to a file and brought out the papers. "There's his signature . . . there and there. I'll take this sheet and get Jenny out there to send it with a wee note. Care for a dram while we're waiting? I've got to walk the dog."

Jenny having been given her instructions, they went to a bar in the Castle Wynd and drank whisky and chatted amiably about various cases. "Drink up," said Mr. Brand at last. "Should be a reply by now."

They went back to the office, where the laconic Jenny produced a fax from the bank confirming the fact that the signature was genuine. Hamish felt he should have been pleased and relieved that Peter Hynd was obviously alive and kicking, but he felt strangely let down. He went back out into the street and stood irresolute.

"Hullo there!" He found Sophy Bisset smiling up at him.

"What brings you to Inverness?" asked Hamish.

"I had to go to the dentist. Had the most awful toothache," said Sophy. "What about you?"

Hamish remembered walking into the hotel reception with Priscilla and telling her where he was going while Sophy had leaned on the reception desk, listening to every word, but he said briefly he had been investigating something.

"I was thinking of making a day of it and having lunch and going to a movie," said Sophy. "Care to join me?"

Hamish hesitated. He had not told Strathbane he was going to Inverness, but he was hardly ever called on the car radio and he had left the answering machine switched on at the police station.

He was suddenly weary of the awkward situation with Priscilla. "All right," he said.

They had lunch in a self-service restaurant and then went round to the small cinema. The film, *Blood and Lust,* was violent and pornographic. There was nothing, reflected Hamish, like a really pornographic film for making a man feel that celibacy was a good idea. Who liked watching other people making love, apart from perverts? He voiced this thought aloud to Sophy, who burst out laughing and told him he belonged in the Dark Ages. But Hamish felt jaded and grimy. It transpired that Sophy had arrived by bus and train, so he politely offered her a lift home although he longed to be by himself.

As he drove out of Inverness, he switched on the police radio. The crackling voices reminded him of his professional status and he was aware that he should not have been carrying a passenger. Then he heard his own name. A peremptory voice told him to get over to Drim, where a death had been reported.

Cursing, he switched on the siren and headed for the Struie Pass and hurtled over the hairpin bends and down into Sutherland. At Bonar Bridge he saw the local bus, which would eventually call at Lochdubh, and skidded to a halt. "You'll need to take the bus, Sophy," he said. "I'm going to be in trouble as it is."

Again she kissed him on the cheek and Hamish was aware of watching eyes from the bus as he recognized the startled faces of the Currie sisters.

He swung off on the road that would take him over the hills to Drim.

O Village of Death, was his thought as he drove down and saw the huddle of villagers by the black loch, the forensic men in their boiler suits, the flashing blue lights of the police cars.

"Where the fuck were you, laddie?" demanded Blair when Hamish walked up. Hamish briefly explained about Peter Hynd.

"You had no right to go off yer patch an no' give us a report," howled Blair. "Start by asking some of these yokels if they know anything."

Hamish turned his back on him and said to Blair's sidekick, Jimmy Anderson, "Who's dead?"

"Betty Baxter."

"Where's the child, Heather?"

"Being looked after at the manse. Mrs. Baxter was found face-down beside the loch, behind that clump of rock. It could be an accident. It looks as if she might have tripped and fallen so hard that she broke her neck."

Hamish walked forward. The tent which had shielded the body had been taken away. The pathologist was stripping off his gloves and packing his bag. A police photographer was taking shots of the body.

Betty Baxter lay in an ungainly pose, diminished by death. Hamish noticed that her hair had been recently blonded, no dark roots, and that she was wearing those silly high heels.

"Accident?" he asked the pathologist.

He shook his head slowly. "I'll have a better idea when I get the body back to the mortuary." He bent over the body. "See here, she's got a huge bruise on her forehead. Looks at first as if she tripped on those silly heels and fell heavily. She's a big woman. But here at the back of the neck there's a big bruise under the hair. Someone came up behind her and struck her hard, a powerful blow with something like a blackjack or lead pipe."

"A man?"

"A woman could have done it with the right weapon."

Hamish walked back to Jimmy Anderson. "No clues?"

"None so far. Ye cannae get footprints from the pebbles on thon beach."

"What about the husband, Harry?"

"No time of death yet. But he was out at the fishing all night, and then this morning, which is when it was guessed she was killed, Harry was in the bar at Lochdubh, seen by God knows how many of your neighbours. We've been over to Lochdubh. Blair's setting up interviews in the community hall.

What do you know about the situation here, Hamish?"

Haish rapidly told him about his seemingly unfounded suspicions about the absent Peter Hynd.

"Well, he cannae be a suspect," said Anderson, "for no one's seen hide nor hair of him since he left that note with Jock."

"How do you know about the note he left with Jock?"

"I asked around if there had been any trouble in the village and some fellow told me that this Hynd and Jock had had a fight." Blair called Anderson sharply.

Both men, followed by Blair's other sidekick, MacNab, and several policemen, headed off to the community hall.

Hamish walked along to the manse. Annie Duncan answered the door. "I don't want Heather pestered," she said quickly. "Just a few words," said Hamish soothingly. "Where's Harry?"

"I gather her father is at home. Could you not leave it to another day? I don't think Heather is up to this."

The small figure of Heather materialized at Annie's elbow. "I will speak to Mr. Macbeth," she said.

Annie reluctantly stood back and Hamish followed them into the kitchen. Heather sat down at the table and Hamish sat opposite her. Annie stood behind the little girl, her hands on her shoulders.

"Do you know when your mother went out?" asked Hamish.

"I got up at seven," said Heather, "and she'd left me a note on the kitchen table to say she had gone out and to get myself ready for school."

"Have you got that note?"

"I threw it away."

"Can you think of any reason why she might have gone out?"

Heather's grey eyes surveyed him thoughtfully and then she said, "Yesterday morning, before Da came home, she got a phone call. I couldna' hear what she said. But she went straight to the hairdresser. She neffer went to the hairdresser for my da."

For a moment it was almost as if Peter Hynd were in the kitchen with them, his eyes dancing with mockery.

"Did you tell the other policemen this?"

"Thon big fat scunner came tae ask me questions. I didn't like him so I told him nothing." Heather got up from the table. "Thank you, Mrs. Duncan. I'll be off home now."

Annie looked distressed. "But you must stay here. My husband will be home shortly and he will want a word with you."

Heather suddenly looked as old as the hills. "To pray ower me? There is no God. Mr. Macbeth, perhaps you will come with me?"

"Yes," said Hamish. He looked at Annie. "I think she will find out what's best for herself."

"My da will need me now," said Heather. "I'll get my stuff."

"She is in shock," said Annie, distressed. "If only she would break down and cry and get it over with. I feel so helpless."

"I'll keep an eye on her," said Hamish. "I wonder if that was Peter Hynd on the phone. Had Betty been dressed up since he left?"

"No, like the rest of the women, she had begun to let herself go. But Mr. Hynd, Peter, was — is — a very sophisticated young man, and although it amused him to flirt with the village women, he would hardly creep back from wherever he's gone to meet Betty Baxter. Nor would he murder her."

"What makes you so sure of that?"

"He was too easygoing."

"So who do you think did it?"

"It's usually the husband, isn't it?"

"But Harry Baxter evidently has a cast-iron alibi for the time of the murder."

She gave a weary shrug, "It could yet turn out to be an unfortunate accident. Passions can run high in this village. But murder! Probably some mad hiker came across her."

"And the phone call?"

"I would be careful about believing anything Heather says at the moment. She is in shock."

At that moment Heather walked into the kitchen carrying a duffle bag over one thin shoulder.

She and Hamish said goodbye to the minister's wife and walked out and along the side of the loch, which lay black and silent and still. Then they cut off up the hill, both avoiding looking along the shore where the white suits of the forensic team gleamed in the twilight.

"Nights are drawing in," said Hamish. "It seems to get verra dark all at once."

"This ae nighte, this ae nighte,
— Every nighte and alle,
Fire and fleet and candle-lighte,
And Christe receive thy saule."

Her childish voice piping the words of the old Lyke-Wake Dirge gave Hamish a shudder. "Read much?" he asked.

"All the time," said Heather. "Books are better'n people any day."

"What have you read recently?"

"I read all Walter Scott's novels this summer."

Hamish was amazed to hear that anyone read Walter Scott's novels in this day and age. "I'll see if I can bring you over some books tomorrow," he said.

At Harry Baxter's house, there was a policeman on duty outside. "Harry home?" asked Hamish.

"Aye, he's in there. Blair's coming back to see him."

Hamish and Heather went inside. Harry was slumped at the kitchen table, his face grey. A glass of whisky stood in front of him.

"That will not do, Da," said Heather, dropping her bag to the floor. "Food and sweet tea is what you need." She picked up the glass of whisky and tipped the contents down the sink.

Hamish sat down next to Harry. "Bad business," he said.

Harry shook his head from side to side. "Who waud have done sich a thing?"

"You'll need to brace up for Heather's sake," said Hamish.

"I'll manage if you keep that bastard, Blair, away from me," said Harry wearily.

Heather had put a frying-pan on the stove and was frying bacon and eggs.

There was a knock at the door. "I'll get it," said Heather quickly.

Then they could hear Blair's heavy voice, "I'm just going to have another word with your faither."

"Begone!" said Heather. "This is a house of mourning and you are harassing and tormenting a poor child."

"Aw, come on, it's your da I want tae see."

"I see the gentleman of the press have arrived," came Heather's voice, "and I will be telling them how you victimized a child of twelve!"

"Och, I'll be back." Blair's voice, thick with disgust and anger. "Hamish Macbeth's in there."

"Mr. Macbeth is a friend." Then came the slamming of the door. Heather returned sedately to the cooker and flipped the eggs.

"I think I'd better be going, Harry. You'd best get one of the women to help you with Heather."

"I don't need anyone," said Heather. "Da and I are best left alone."

Hamish went out, puzzled. He had never met anyone like Heather before. He wondered if Priscilla could make anything of her.

He decided that instead of going to the community hall to interview the villagers himself, he would start off with the hairdresser, Alice MacQueen, and find out if Betty had said anything. Alice MacQueen had already suffered being interviewed by Blair and it took Hamish some time to soothe her ruffled feathers. She was a faded woman with small features and a pinched mouth. Her dark-brown hair was worn in the old-fashioned chrysanthemum style she inflicted on her customers and highlighted with streaks of silver.

Her "shop" was in her converted front-room and smelled of chemicals and hot hair. "What I am trying to find out from you, you being obviously a verra sensitive and noticing sort of lady, is if Betty Baxter, when she had her hair done, seemed any different from usual."

"Well, she talked a lot, but then she always did." Alice wrinkled her brow. "But she looked . . . triumphant. She looked as if there was some secret she was hugging. Maybe found herself another fellow."

"Not Peter Hynd?"

She snorted. "Him? He's long gone. Anyway, he wasn't interested in Betty. She ran after him like a great cow."

Hamish asked more questions and then

gave up. The one satisfaction he had was that this murder investigation would lead to finding out where Peter Hynd was. Although he had left the village, the police would want to ask him if he had any idea who might have killed Betty.

He was about to go up to Jimmy Macleod's house when Jimmy Anderson came running up just as Hamish was leaving the hairdresser's. "Looks like an accident after all," he said.

"What? What about that bruise on her neck?"

"Blair's jist got that out o' her man. That wee Heather tells Blair her father has something to say. Seems Harry skelped her one with a half-frozen cod on the back of the neck yesterday when he saw she'd been back to the hairdresser to get blonded."

"But what broke her neck then?"

"It was a freak accident. It was the way she fell among the rocks. She's got a broken arm as well. Pathologist made a second examination before they took the body away."

"Has he gone? I want a word with him."

"He's gone and everyone else is packing up."

"Just like that? Okay, so Harry hit her with a cod, but couldn't someone have pushed her — deliberately pushed her hard onto the rocks?"

"No use trying to talk me into seeing it as murder. I jist want tae get to the pub afore they close. Try Blair."

"Have better success talking to Harry's cod."

Hamish went up to the row of police cars. Blair was laughing uproariously at something one of the policewomen had said. His piggy eyes fastened on Hamish and he scowled. "Jist as well it was an accident, Hamish, or there'd be an inquiry about why ye were neglecting your duties and had the radio switched off."

"You mean like Dolan's inquiry?"

"None of your lip!"

"Look," said Hamish earnestly, "why are you all so eager to accept the diagnosis of accident? The woman was obviously going to meet someone. She had a phone call, she got her hair bleached, and she was all dressed up."

"Och, who can tell what goes on in the crazy minds of these teuchters," said Blair, who hailed from Glasgow and considered all Highlanders barbarians. "I'm telling ye, it was an accident plain and simple."

"At least find out where Peter Hynd went and ask him some questions."

"The case is closed. It's different fur you layabouts. We've got murder and mayhem daily in Strathbane."

Hamish made a disgusted sound and went back to the Baxters' house. The press had gone, the policeman had gone. He knocked at the door. It was opened a crack and Heather's grey eyes peered out. She saw Hamish and opened the door wide. "Da's gone to bed," she said.

"Heather, I don't want to distress you further, but what's all this about your father hitting your mother with a codfish?"

"It wass yesterday," she said in a singsong voice, and he was forcibly reminded of a good child reciting poetry at a school function. "She wass standing by the cooker and they had a quarrel. That's when it happened."

"Why didn't you tell me this before?"

"Da thought he would get into trouble, but I told him it wass better to tell the truth."

Hamish eyed her narrowly. "You wouldn't make up a story to protect your father, would you, Heather, and find you were protecting a murderer instead?"

"I don't lie," she said fiercely.

Hamish went back to the police Land Rover and sat in it, moodily staring down at the loch. He felt that if he did not investigate this case further, it would nag at him until the day he died. Yes, he was lazy, but the taking of human life was the ultimate crime and he could not believe Betty's death had been an accident.

He was due a three weeks' holiday. His bank account was showing a modest sum of money. He had planned to take Priscilla on holiday. He struck the steering wheel. But what would the fair Priscilla say when he asked her? What would she think as a vision of the intimacy of a hotel bedroom rose in her cold mind? But he made up his mind. He would drive back and ask her. If she refused, then he would use the holiday to find Peter Hynd.

He drove out of Drim and straight to the Tommel Castle Hotel. There had been a special reception and dinner for the new guests. When he went in, they were in the bar, Priscilla among them in a flame-coloured silk dress, laughing and talking with two of the men. The men were worldly, expensive- and sophisticated-looking in their evening dress. He felt suddenly gawky and ill at ease. Priscilla looked up and saw him, and the laughter left her face and her eyes took on a guarded look. She walked up to him. "Hamish?"

"Can we talk?"

"I'm very busy," she said coolly. "Oh, come into the office."

They walked into the hotel office. "Now, Hamish," said Priscilla briskly.

"It iss not the business meeting," retorted Hamish huffily. "I've decided to take a three weeks' holiday, and I thought we could just pack up and go somewhere."

"Just like that?"

"Why not?"

"What were you doing driving Sophy Bisset back from Inverness? And I gather you had a splendid time having lunch and going to watch a dirty movie."

"Priscilla, I told you I was going to Inverness. I happened to run into Sophy, that was all. Then I heard about the death at Drim and dropped her at the bus stop at Bonar Bridge. No doubt the Currie sisters reported it all."

"Not to mention Sophy herself."

"I'm telling you, there wass nothing to it." His Highland accent was becoming more sibilant, a sign that he was upset. "Let's not quarrel. Let's talk about this holiday."

"I cannot possibly go off on holiday now. We are too busy."

"Priscilla, you'll need to chuck the hotel work when we're married."

"Why? We'll need the money," she said brutally. "Have you any idea what a dress like this costs?" Priscilla knew she was behaving badly, and like most hurt people was taking a vindictive pleasure in it. "When we are married, *if* we are married, then I shall get Pa to pay me a salary. I do the work of two, sometimes more. Then there's the gift shop to run."

"I have no intention of living off my wife's earnings," said Hamish stiffly.

"Why am I so different?" she asked sweetly. "You mooch off everyone else in Lochdubh."

He looked at her with sudden hatred. "You," he said evenly, "are a thoroughly nasty bitch!"

Hamish turned on his heel and walked out.

Priscilla stood for a long moment after he had gone and then sat down at the desk and burst into tears.

"Hamish! Hamish!" He turned round in the car-park. Sophy came running towards him. "Everything all right?" she asked.

He looked at her with loathing. "Go and jump in the loch," he said rudely. "Women! They should all be strangled at birth!"

He climbed into the Land Rover and

drove off, gravel spurting out from under his wheels.

It was only when he was back in his own kitchen with only the company of Towser that he began to calm down. He could not go over and over what Priscilla had said, picking away at the hurt like a scab. In the morning he would go to Strathbane and make arrangements for his holiday.

And then he would set out to find Peter Hynd.

He went down to Strathbane the next day and obtained permission to take leave. Sergeant Macgregor over at Cnothan would cover Hamish's beat as well as his own. That finished, Hamish returned to Lochdubh, collected Towser and took the dog over to his parents' home in Rogart, where he shrugged off questions about his wedding date with, he thought, very clever answers. His mother sadly watched him driving off and said to her husband, "I don't think our Hamish is going to marry Priscilla or anyone. He always was a picky boy."

Hamish then returned to Lochdubh and arranged with a neighbour to take care of his hens and sheep. He had already made up his mind to go to London and see if he could trace the origins of Peter Hynd. First he would need some money. As he walked to the bank, he suddenly realized that Peter Hynd must have had some local bank he drew money from. There was no bank in Drim.

He walked in and asked to see the bank manager, a new man called Ian Donaldson. He had to wait twenty minutes. The recession had reached the north of Scotland in that the banks were calling in loans and managers were besieged by furious customers.

The bank manager rose to meet him. "Well, Macbeth, I hope you havenae come for a loan, for I amn't giving any."

"Nothing like that," said Hamish. "That young chap, Peter Hynd, him that was over at Drim. Did he use this bank?"

"Aye, from time to time."

"Had an arrangement with you?"

"Nothing like that. Just cashed the odd cheque for fifty pounds and paid the fee. So much plastic around these days, people don't need cash in hand like they used to."

"Got any of those cheques?"

"No, he hasn't been in here for a few weeks, so the cheques will have already been sent on to his own bank in New Bond Street. Why? He isn't a criminal, is he?"

"Just following up some inquiries," said Hamish.

He drew out money and then hesitated outside the bank. It was a glorious early-autumn day. The heather had settled down to a rusty colour and the rowan-trees were heavy with scarlet berries. The fishing boats were mirrored in the loch. Smoke rose in straight lines from chimneys. The air was full of homely noises: women calling to each other as they hung out the washing, snatches of radio, the grinding of a rusty winch down at the harbour, the chanting voices of the children in the schoolroom reciting the multiplication table.

As he surveyed the scene, he had a longing to forget about useless Peter Hynd and stay in Lochdubh and laze the days away, get in a bit of fishing, read, and watch television. But as he viewed the loch, a pleasure launch came into view, the Tommel Castle Hotel's latest acquisition. It was full of guests and he could make out Priscilla's blonde hair.

With a little sigh, he went back to the police station and began to pack.

His cousin, Rory Grant, a reporter on a national daily newspaper, was not amused to find Hamish complete with suitcase on his doorstep. "This isn't a hotel, Hamish," he said. "I could have had a woman here."

"But you haven't," said the unrepentant Hamish, walking in and putting his suitcase in the middle of the floor. "I'm only here for a wee bit, and if you're any help to me, I'll let you in on a good story."

"Like what?"

Hamish told him about Peter Hynd.

"Sounds a bit far-fetched to me," said Rory. "If you want free board, just say so."

"No, I mean it. I really want to find him."

"Okay, your room's through here. Look, I think I'm on to a sure thing tonight, Hamish. There's this woman reporter on the *Sun* . . . well, you know how it is. I'm taking her out for dinner and I think I might score. We're going to a restaurant in South Ken, Bernie's Bistro. I've got to go into the office, so I'll see if there's anything on Peter Hynd on file. If you drop in at the restaurant at eight, say, I'll give you anything I've got, but don't stay, for heaven's sake. Take yourself off and get some fish and chips or something."

"I'll do that," said Hamish, suddenly feeling more cheerful. "I'll start off at his bank in New Bond Street."

"How's Priscilla?"

"Chust fine."

"Did well for yourself, Hamish. Wish I could marry into a rich family."

Hamish paused in the act of opening his suitcase. "I haff no intention of using my wife's money or her family's money."

"Ballocks. Get real, as our American cousins say. Wake up and smell the coffee. Victorian values don't apply in a recession. I'm telling you, if I get a rich wife, I'll chuck reporting and sit on my bum pretending to write the great novel while wifie pays the bills without one qualm of conscience."

"Aye, well, London's corrupted you. I will do fine if you want to get off."

"I'll get your door keys first," said Rory. "You know where everything is. Don't forget, Bernie's Bistro. Come out of South Ken tube, turn right, and it's a few yards along once you cross the intersection."

"I'll find it. And thanks, Rory."

Rory grinned and with his lanky figure and red hair suddenly looked very much like Hamish. He waved and went out. Hamish hung away his clothes and, still feeling stiff and groggy after a night on the train, went out into the streets of Kensington. Rory's flat was in a converted building right on the Gloucester Road. The day was crisp and fine and he decided to walk to Bond Street through Kensington Gardens, then Hyde Park, and so along Piccadilly and down Bond Street.

He felt more relaxed than he had for some time.

The hunt for Peter Hynd had begun in earnest.

CHAPTER 7

Even if we take matrimony at its lowest,
even if we regard it as no more than a sort
of friendship recognised by the police.
                          Robert Louis Stevenson

Hamish left the bank feeling puzzled. Peter
Hynd certainly had an account with them
but no money had been drawn by him
anywhere in the last few weeks. But he had
a London address in the Vale of Health,
Hampstead. He went into Fenwick's, the
Bond Street department store, and up to
the coffee shop and examined the tube map
at the back of his diary while he drank coffee, the only man in a roomful of women.

He made his way out into a street, which
looked strangely thin of people compared to
the bustling main street of Inverness, say,
walked to Bond Street Tube and took the
Central Line to Tottenham Court Road, and
changed to the Northern Edgware Line. It

took him an hour to reach Hampstead. He was always amazed at the vastness of London, although the infrequent trains on the Northern Line always served to slow up any journey. Thriftily not wanting to spend any more money than he had to, he walked into a Hampstead newsagent's, took down a London A-Z, located the Vale of Health, and returned the book to the shelf.

The Vale of Health, originally called Hackett's Bottom, nestled in a hollow of the Heath beside a pond. As he walked down the twisting road, he saw a small fairground in front of the houses and beyond that the trees and grass and walks of Hampstead Heath.

Peter Hynd's house was a trim villa in a terrace of villas, painted ice-cream pink. Much as he disliked Peter Hynd, as Hamish pressed the bell, he wished with all his heart and soul that the man himself would answer the door. But it was a rather bizarre young woman who looked up at him, her dusty hair backcombed and left that way, making her look like some cartoon about electric-shock therapy. Her skin was sallow and she wore old-fashioned purple lipstick and her tired eyes were rimmed with kohl.

"Mr. Hynd?" asked Hamish. "I am from the Sutherland police," he added, thinking that sounded grander than Lochdubh.

"What's it about?"

"Is he here?"

"No, he's somewhere up your part of the world. Oh, I suppose you know that. He's our landlord."

"And when did you see him last?"

She crinkled her brow and then shouted over her shoulder, "Clive!"

A squat bald man, or, as Hamish supposed one would have to say these days, one of the follicly disadvantaged, hove into view.

"This man's from the police," she said. "He's asking about Peter."

"Good God, woman. When will you ever learn? Some fellow turns up on the doorstep and claims to be a policeman and you don't even ask to see any identification."

"Well, I did, so get stuffed," she said, throwing Hamish a conspiratorial wink. Clive made a disgusted sound and walked away.

"Brownie points to me," she said cheerfully. "Never let the bastards get the upper hand, husbands, I mean." She cocked her head to one side. "He's gone upstairs. Come down to the kitchen and have a cup of coffee. You've come a long way, so it must be important. Although I didn't ask you for any identification, I trust you not to be the rapist of Hampstead Heath, although," her eyes slanted mockingly at him, "on the other hand, this might be my lucky day."

Hamish followed her downstairs to a cheerful kitchen hung with a couple of braces of pheasant and a hare. "Early for the pheasant, not October yet," said Hamish.

"Oh, them? They're stuffed. Got a lot of twee friends who go in for exotic cooking. When they see the game hanging up, they never guess what I'm serving them came from the restaurant up the road. Got to keep one's end up. Clive is with the Beeb."

"The Beeb?"

"The BBC."

"What does he do?"

"He produces a programme called 'Culture For Everyman.' He loves it. He gets to patronize the great British public once a week. How do you like your coffee?"

"Just black with a spoon of sugar."

"Right you are. I'm Jill Cadden. I'm in films."

"I didn't think there was a film industry left in Britain," commented Hamish.

"Well, it's a small experimental company. We're politically motivated."

"Tell me about Peter," said Hamish. "I

176

mean, don't you see him to give him the rent?"

"No, we pay him by standing order. Goes from our bank to his every month."

"How much does he charge?"

"Thirteen hundred a month."

"Pounds!"

"Hardly be dollars or Deutschmarks, would it? And that's pretty reasonable for this size of house and garden in this neck of the woods."

"Wouldn't it be cheaper to buy a wee place and pay the mortgage?" asked Hamish curiously.

"You see, it . . ." Jill looked at him with amusement. "How do you ever get to the point, copper? Or does life move slower in Sutherland? What's Peter been up to?"

"He was living in the village of Drim up on the northwest coast. He left and put his cottage up for sale. But no one saw him leave. Then a woman's been found dead. It's been said it wass the accident," said Hamish, becoming worried again as in his mind's eye he saw Betty Baxter's ungainly dead body sprawled on the cruel rocks, "but I am not so sure."

"You're thorough, I'll say that," said Jill, handing him a cup of coffee. "It seems you think that Peter had something to do with this woman's death or that he has been killed himself."

"Something like that," said Hamish. "What did you think of Peter?"

A shuttered look came down over her eyes. "All right. Bit lightweight. Not much there. What you see is what you get."

"Would you say he was manipulative?"

"We only rented the house from him. We didn't go into any deep psychoanalysis." Her voice was tetchy.

"Any family? This is his house, not a family home?"

"Yes, it's his house. He has a sister somewhere, I believe."

"He never said anything about his family? Where they lived, where he went to school?"

She yawned. "We weren't buddies. He's just a landlord, that's all."

Hamish could get little out of her but he left with a feeling that Jill had been subject to Peter's philandering tactics.

He would need to wait and see if Rory had found anything on the newspaper files.

As he walked up and away from the Vale of Health, he began to worry whether he had merely used this investigation as an excuse to run away from Priscilla. He sometimes wondered which one of them was really at fault. He debated whether to call in at New Scotland Yard and ask if they had anything on Peter Hynd on their files. But Scotland Yard would phone Strathbane to check his credentials and then he would be on the carpet for trying to play the part of private detective in London.

Priscilla drove down to the police station. This quarrel was silly. Sophy Bisset was a very pushy sort of girl and Hamish was putty in the hands of pushy girls. She must put the treacherous thought that Hamish Macbeth was putty in the hands of any female out of her mind.

The police station was locked up and a notice on the door referred all inquiries to Sergeant Macgregor at Cnothan for the next three weeks. Where had Hamish gone? She had never known him to take a real holiday, apart from that free one at the health farm, which had ended up in a murder inquiry anyway.

His parents! He was bound to have gone to Rogart to spend some time with his family. She drove to Rogart and received a noisy welcome from Towser. Mrs. Macbeth shook her head and said Hamish was off investigating something, that was all she knew.

So Priscilla stayed for tea and left saddened by the fact that Hamish's name and her marriage prospects were not mentioned, although the air had been thick with un-asked questions.

As she drove home, she began to become angry with him. How dare he go off like that without even calling on her? Yes, they had had a row. All couples had rows. But he should have understood that she could not just pack up, just like that, and go with him on holiday. Wherever he was, she sincerely hoped, and from the bottom of her heart, that he was missing her like hell and having a dreadful time.

Hamish made his way along to Bernie's Bistro. He was wearing his civilian outfit of sports jacket, corduroy trousers, checked shirt, and tie. He wondered uneasily whether he should have put on a dark suit, the one he kept for church services, funerals, and weddings. He pushed open the door of the restaurant and went in. He saw Rory right away. He was sitting at a corner table wearing jeans and a pullover over a T-shirt, so formal dress did not seem to be the order of the day. "I'm waiting for Mandy," said Rory. "The girl from the *Sun.* She's late, but then she always is."

Hamish sat down and looked eagerly at his cousin. "Find out anything?"

"Nothing much. One little snippet. There's a fashionable London night-club called Tarts. Heard of it?"

"No."

"Never mind. Home to the glitterati. There was a scene there two years ago. A young starlet got drunk and tried to set the place on fire. Police called. Her escort was one Peter Hynd, described as an Old Westminster and socialite. Might be your man. No photo."

"What's an Old Westminster?"

"Former pupil of Westminster School, down by the Abbey. Expensive fees. Brightest and best. Highest academic rating in the country. Goes back to the time of the founder, Queen Elizabeth the First. Former pupils, Christopher Wren, Philby, and Peter Ustinov. You got a photo of this Peter Hynd?"

Hamish shook his head.

"Well, trot down there tomorrow and ask the registrar. The office is in Little Dean's, off Dean's Yard. Find the Abbey and you can't miss it. Oh, here's Mandy."

A plumpish girl in a short leather skirt and suede jacket had just come in. She had short spiky hair, a turned-up nose, and a wide mouth.

She kissed Rory on the cheek and then

sat down and looked at Hamish. "Screw all news editors," she said. "Who's this?"

"My cousin Hamish, down from the Highlands. He's just leaving."

"Why?"

"Because this is our date."

"You can't send your cousin away," said Mandy, delighted at the prospect of having two men beside her for dinner. "Let's all eat together."

"I really must be going," said Hamish, receiving the full blast of a fulminating glare from Rory.

Mandy smiled into his eyes. "My treat."

Hamish was very hungry. There were delicious smells of food all about him. Avoiding Rory's eyes, he said, "Maybe I'll just stay for a little."

Rory tried to talk newspaper shop and so exclude Hamish from the conversation, but Mandy plied Hamish with questions about his work in Scotland. It was only half-way through the meal that he realized she had the newspaper reporter's off-duty trick of asking a lot of questions and not really listening to the answers. "Look, I am a reporter and I ask incisive questions," she seemed to be saying. Whatever Hamish replied to those questions was of little interest compared to Mandy's interest in her own personality — or rather the one she had knitted for herself. His appetite satisfied, he wished he had not stayed. Mandy's main intention was to make Rory jealous and she had initially succeeded in doing just that. But by the time the pudding was served, Hamish could see Rory was growing bored.

He glanced at his watch and manufactured a look of shock. "I'd quite forgotten, I've got to meet a fellow," he said, pushing his plate away and getting to his feet. Rory followed him to the restaurant door. "Look, you great pillock," he said. "Don't balls up any more of this evening. Wander the streets, do anything, but don't turn up at the flat until I've got this one safely into bed."

"I'm sorry, Rory, but I was hungry."

"Make up for it. Don't come home until the small hours."

Hamish left the restaurant and set out towards the West End. He went to the late show of a movie and then went to an all-night café and drank coffee and watched the clock until he thought it was safe to return.

He crept into the flat and made his way to his room. He undressed and washed and climbed into bed. Sounds of noisy activity were coming from the next room. He pulled the blankets over his head and wished he were back in the police station in Lochdubh.

In the morning he went down to Westminster School. He marvelled that such a quiet backwater could exist in the heart of London. The various school houses were grouped around a quadrangle, Little Dean's. Virginia creeper flamed on the old walls of Ashburnham House. Boys in the school uniform of charcoal-grey suit and plain blue tie crossed and recrossed Little Dean's on their way to and from classes. One of them directed him to the registrar's office.

He patiently explained to the registrar his name, profession, and interest in Peter Hynd. Files were checked and then the registrar said, "The best thing you can do is to pay a visit on Peter's old housemaster. He left two years ago and is living in Madingley Road in Cambridge. Here's the address. His name is Mr. James Heath."

Cambridge! Hamish was tempted to forget about the whole thing and return to Lochdubh. Still . . .

"How do I get there?" he asked.

Armed with instructions, he took the tube from St. James's to Liverpool Street Station and caught the Cambridge train. With the aid of a map drawn for him by the registrar, he walked from the station at Cambridge to Madingley Road. He began to worry that he should have phoned first. In fact, he could probably just have interviewed this Mr. Heath on the phone. He found the address, a big Victorian building divided into flats, and pressed the bell over a neat card marked "J. Heath."

To his relief, a buzzer sounded and he went into a large dark hall checkered with coloured light from the stained-glass panel on the door. An authoritative voice called, "Up here. First landing."

Hamish went up the stairs. Mr. Heath was waiting for him. He was a thin, spare man with a clever, humorous face. Hamish rapidly explained he was from the Sutherland police and wanted to make certain inquiries about Peter Hynd. Mr. Heath threw him a quizzical look but said, "Come in. Sit yourself down. Tea or coffee?"

"Tea," said Hamish, thinking he had drunk enough coffee the night before to last him a lifetime.

While the ex-housemaster made tea, Hamish crossed the book-lined room and stood by the window and looked across to the spires of Cambridge. The rattling of teacups made him turn round as Mr. Heath came in, carrying a loaded tray which contained not only teapot and cups but fruit-cake and sandwiches.

"Now," said Mr. Heath when they were comfortably settled by the fire, "what's all this about Peter?"

Hamish said briefly that Peter had been resident in the village of Drim and had left, he felt, under suspicious circumstances. "I mean, it's the Highlands of Scotland," said Hamish. "You would think someone would have seen him leave. What did you make of his character?"

A slightly guarded look came into the housemaster's eyes. "He was a boarder. Westminster takes day boys as well. I always thought he had been sent to the wrong school."

"In what way?"

"The boys who come to us are usually very bright. The fees are high and people who do not know Westminster assume it is a school, like Eton, for the privileged, but a lot of our pupils are very gifted and there is not much emphasis on sport. I think Peter felt out of place."

"Was he very manipulative?" asked Hamish.

"An odd question."

"Well, was he?" There was a long silence and then Mr. Heath said, "It's not as if you are from the newspapers. Yes, he was. At first he seemed quite bright, but I found he had got a hold of some kind over some of the boys and was making them do his homework for him. He craved attention and admiration. One teacher who gave him a hard time immediately became the butt of scurrilous gossip. I thought Peter was behind it but could prove nothing. The worst thing he did was with the girls."

"How? This is important."

"We have girls in the final years. He was a remarkably beautiful boy. He enjoyed setting one girl against the other. One of our most brilliant girls failed her exams because she was so besotted with him."

Hamish drew a long breath. "Peter Hynd moved into the village of Drim," he said. "The young people have mostly left for the cities, but the middle-aged women fell hook, line, and sinker for Peter. He made sure that's exactly what they would do. The atmosphere in the village was terrible, full of hate and menace. Recently, one of the women, Betty Baxter, was found dead on the beach, her neck broken, diagnosed as accident, but I'm not so sure. Now, would you say he could engender enough hate for someone to murder him?"

"Oh, yes," said Mr. Heath calmly. "I felt

like murdering him myself."

"Does he have a family? Where does the money come from?"

"The parents are both dead. The fees were paid by a family trust. He has a sister, an elder sister. She used to come on parents' day. Now what was her name? Beth, that was it, Beth Hynd. She may have married by now. Lived in Richmond. Peter spent his school holidays with her. I am afraid I cannot remember the address."

As he left, Hamish groaned inwardly. Back to London and then Richmond. He had meant to stay and look around Cambridge, but the desire to prove to himself that he was not on a wild-goose chase, that he had not wasted his holidays, drove him on. He was fortunate in catching a fast train and an hour later was back in London and on the tube to Richmond.

Richmond, which he had not visited before, was much larger and sprawling than he had expected. He did not want to enlist the help of the local police and so draw attention to himself. But where to start? He went into the nearest post office and asked for the telephone directory. Women no longer prefixed their names in the phone books with "Miss" or "Mrs." for fear of getting obscene calls. Her first name would be

Elizabeth, he thought, turning the pages, so it would probably be under E. Hynd. There were several E. Hynds in the Richmond area, so he bought a phone card and went out to the box and began to phone each one.

At the third call, just when he was beginning to think she might have an ex-directory number, Beth Hynd answered the phone. She listened to him carefully and then said cautiously that he could call on her but to have his identification ready and to tell her before he arrived a number in Sutherland she could call to confirm he was who he said he was. Hamish gave her Jimmy Anderson's name and the Strathbane number. He rang off, put the card back in the slot, and dialled Strathbane police headquarters. To his infinite relief, Jimmy Anderson was there. The detective listened while Hamish briefly outlined the reason for his visit south. "Nobody's going to love ye if this turns out tae be murder," said Anderson. "Daviot'll consider you've made a fool o' the lot of us."

"Don't care," said Hamish. "Chust tell this woman I am who I am."

"Right you are, Popeye."

Hamish left the box, realizing he had not asked Beth for directions. He went into a newsagent's and consulted a street directory and found that the street in which she lived was not very far away.

Although Beth Hynd was in her late thirties — Hamish judged her to be about ten years older than her brother — there was a strong family likeness. She also reminded him forcibly of someone he had met recently.

She invited him into the living-room of her home. It was a pleasant-enough room, well-ordered, but lit with a 40-watt bulb behind one of those old-fashioned glass shades, which gave the place the air of the type of waiting-room one waits in before some humiliation — dentist, gynaecologist, headmaster — or the lounge of an old folks' home where the elderly sit and play Scrabble and wait for death's bright angel to pop his head round the door and say, "Come in, Number Six, your time's up." An old-fashioned gas fire hissed and popped.

"I trust Peter has come to no harm," she said.

Hamish had no intention of scaring her with a belief that Peter Hynd might have been murdered. "I am investigating a death in the village of Drim," he said, "where your brother lived . . ."

"Lived? You mean he is not still there?"

"No, he left a few weeks ago. I judged him

to be a clever young man who might have seen something that the locals missed. Do you know where he is?"

She shook her head.

"He usually turns up here sooner or later. I will tell him to phone you immediately when he arrives."

"Does he work at anything?"

"He took various jobs, but as he has a private income he does not need to work and so he never really stuck at anything for very long."

"Any romantic entanglements?"

Her eyes were suddenly sharp. "Why? Why do you ask? What has that got to do with anything?"

Hamish's voice was soothing. "Och, I just thought that if he had a lassie, then she might know where he is."

Her face cleared. "Of course. But I am afraid I know nothing of Peter's love life."

"Where does he live when he's in the south? His house is let."

"Here. He stays here."

"Are you very close?"

A guarded look and then: "Of course. He is my brother."

Hamish stared at her in frustration but he realized there was nothing further to be got out of her. And the room was depressing him. It must be awful, he thought, to have enough private income to knock any idea of getting a job out of one's head.

"What do you do?" he asked.

"Do? I am on the board of a couple of charities. Then there are people to visit. Believe me, there are not enough hours in the day." The sudden loneliness looking out of her eyes belied the statement. Hamish glanced around the room. Books in serried ranks, dark-green house plants, but not even a cat for company.

He found it a relief to be back out in the streets of Richmond, where the air smelled of crisp autumn. He found a cheap restaurant and ate a hamburger and drank Coke with a pleased feeling that Priscilla would disapprove of such junk food.

He would need to get back to the source, he thought, and that was Drim. He felt in his bones that young Heather was right. Peter Hynd was as dead as a doornail, and instead of wasting time in the south, he should be back in the north, asking question after question until a clearer picture appeared. He looked at his watch. If he hurried, he could get back to Rory's, pack up, and catch the night train to Inverness.

He always felt like a fish out of water

investigating things on foreign territory anyway.

As it was, he only managed to leap on the train as it was pulling out. Most of the train consisted of sleeping cars, so he was lucky to find an empty seat in the few carriages allotted to upright passengers.

As he fell asleep, the faces of the women of Drim danced before his eyes. And yet, would it not be more likely that one of the men was the murderer? *Murder, murder, murder,* sang the wheels as the train ploughed north through the darkness, leaving London and the south behind.

"You want *what?*" Jock Kennedy leaned on the counter of his shop and looked in amazement at Hamish Macbeth.

"I want a room," said Hamish patiently.

"Why? You live ower at Lochdubh."

"I'm on my holidays."

"Seems daft tae me. Try Edie Aubrey. She lets out a room tae the tourists."

"Fine."

As Hamish walked to Edie Aubrey's home, he noticed that the community hall now stood silent. He glanced in the window of the hairdresser's as he passed. Alice MacQueen was sitting in a chair by the window, doing her nails. Not a customer in sight.

Two women passed him on their way to the store wearing the inevitable uniform of anorak and ski trousers stretched over massive thighs, lank hair, and no make-up. Nothing anymore to dress up for.

Edie Aubrey looked flustered when he asked for a room. "The season's over," she said nervously. "I haven't aired the room."

"I'm sure it'll do fine," said Hamish.

"Well, it's just bed and breakfast. I don't do any other meals."

"I'll manage."

"Oh, I suppose. You're not here officially then?"

"No, chust wanted to get out of Lochdubh. A policeman's neffer off duty so long as Strathbane knows where he is. Want to get a bit of fishing."

"Follow me," said Edie, apparently making up her mind. The house was one of those many Victorian villas which were built for holidaying English families after Queen Victoria had made the Highlands fashionable. It was small but well-carpeted and well-fired. The bedroom allotted to him contained a large double bed covered in a shiny pink satin quilt. There was one of those old-fashioned basket chairs in a corner, green shot with gold, which held a doll in a frilly dress. Its eyes stared at

Hamish as empty of expression as the dead eyes of Betty Baxter. A large wardrobe dominated one wall, built for the heavier, larger clothes of Victorians. He opened it up. There were shelves on one side for shirts and little drawers for collar studs and dress studs. Over the bed was a picture of two Edwardian girls chasing a small white dog across a field of poppies.

"If you'd like to unpack and come downstairs, I'll make you a cup of tea," said Edie. He smiled at her and she patted her hair and blinked at him through her glasses.

When she had left, Hamish looked out of the window and down to the black expanse of the sea loch. At the far-inland end of the loch, the river Drim fell in peaty brown cascades over jagged rocks. Farther up the river he could see the glint of a pool. He had collected his fishing-rods from the police station before coming to Drim. Perhaps he might go up to that pool and try to get some trout and leave investigations until the morrow. He was supposed to be on holiday, and if the locals really believed that, he might pick up more gossip than he would do if they thought he was in the village on business.

He unpacked and went downstairs. Edie placed a pot of tea and a plate of scones on the table. "You are a widow, aren't you?" asked Hamish.

She poured tea into thick mugs. "Yes, my Jamie passed on ten years ago. He was a fine man."

"You're not from the Highlands?"

"No, from down south. Moffat."

"So what brought you here? These scones are grand."

"Have another. Jamie was ill, cancer. He always thought the Highland air would cure him, thought it right to the last, poor man."

"Didn't you ever want to move back south?"

Edie put down her cup and her eyes strayed to the kitchen window as if seeking the answer among the laurels in the garden. "Oh, I thought of it often. But I didn't have many friends in Moffat, I was too busy looking after Jamie. Somehow I just stayed on here." Her voice was sad. "I've tried to brighten up the place. It was the high moment in my life when they all started coming to the exercise classes. But then Peter left . . ."

Her voice trailed away. "And darkness fell on the land," added Hamish silently.

He finished his tea. Plenty of time for more questions. "I'm just going to take my rod up the Drim and see if I can get any trout."

"I don't usually cook meals, but I'd like a fresh trout for tea. If you catch any, I'll cook them."

"I'll hold you to that."

Hamish almost but not quite forgot the reason for his stay in Drim as he angled in the pool, expertly flicking the fly so that it skimmed on the peaty gold of the water. He had just reeled in his second trout when he had a feeling of being watched. He tipped the trout into the old-fashioned fishing basket he used and turned slowly about. There was a stand of silver birch behind him.

"Come out," he called.

There was a rustling and then the slight figure of Heather Baxter appeared. "You're staying at Mrs. Aubrey's," she said.

"News travels fast," said Hamish. "How are you?"

"Fine, chust fine. Da and I get along well."

Hamish looked at the composed little figure. Would this child kill her own mother so as to have a quiet home and her father to herself? The thought was a repugnant one. It was the fault of the atmosphere of Drim, which easily conjured up Gothic fantasies in the mind.

"Catch anything?" Heather asked.

"Two trout."

"Da would like a trout for his tea, and so would I."

"And so would I," said Hamish. "Sit down over there and I'll see what I can do."

She sat down and clasped her hands over her knees and closed her eyes. Hamish threw her an amused look. "Praying?"

She nodded fiercely and he wondered if she was praying to the Christian God or one of the Celtic pagan ones. To his amazement, he caught his next trout almost immediately. Heather opened her eyes. "And another," she said solemnly and fell to praying again. He cast again but without much success. The day began to grow darker. And then the hair began to rise on his neck, for Heather's voice was rising in a keening sound. He knew she was chanting in Gaelic but he could not make out the exact words. He was about to call to her to stop her nonsense when he felt a tug on the line.

Some minutes later, Heather's voice died away and she looked in satisfaction at the large trout he was landing.

"Come home with me," she said after she had wrapped the present of two trout up in docken leaves. "Mrs. Aubrey's a dreadful cook."

"Off with you," said Hamish, "and don't put your faith in the old gods, Heather. That sort of thing'll turn you potty."

"It got me the trout for Da's tea," said Heather practically, and off she went.

Hamish headed back to the village, carrying his catch. He nodded and said, "Good evening" and "Grand night" to passing villagers, who stopped and stared at him but did not return his greeting.

Edie received the trout with enthusiasm. "I have a new French cookery book," she said, "and there is a very interesting way of baking trout with cheese, so . . ."

"My treat, my cooking," said Hamish firmly. "I'm a dab hand wi' the trout."

He gutted the fish and grilled them and served them with boiled potatoes and peas.

He felt a sudden wave of fatigue. He had not had much sleep on the train north. He cocked his head. A gale was beginning to blow up outside. "I thought you were too sheltered here in Drim to get much wind," he said.

"Oh, we get it all right when it's blowing in from the west," said Edie. "I hate the wind."

The noise outside rose. The wind, channelled down the loch between the tall walls of the mountains, screamed and howled.

It was cosy in the kitchen. The fish were excellent and the potatoes, which turned out to have come from Edie's garden, floury, and almost sweet.

"Strange the way Peter Hynd left," said Hamish, pushing away his empty plate. He groped in his pocket for a packet of cigarettes and then realized with a start that he had given up smoking some time ago.

"Cigarette?" asked Edie, holding out a packet.

For one awful moment he nearly took one. "Given up," he said curtly.

"You don't mind if I . . . ?"

"Go ahead."

Edie lit her cigarette and then said, "The men here were very nasty to Peter. I think that's why he left. You know shortly before he went, someone threw a brick through his window."

"I didn't hear about that!"

"No, well, you wouldn't. You know how they all stick together in these villages."

Hamish looked at her. "Peter Hynd liked to flirt. Was there anyone in particular? Was it just flirting?"

"Ailsa Kennedy was hinting that he had gone further than that with her, but no one really believed her. Then there was Jimmy Macleod's wife, Nancy. Alice MacQueen said she saw her leaving Peter's cottage in the middle of the night, but she would hardly leave her husband's bed to go out in the night without him knowing. Still, it's all over now. The house has been sold."

"What? So soon?"

"Yes, the man from Newcastle and his wife were here early today. A Mr. Apple. He's got the grand plans for building that extension. He's going to move the builders in right away."

"Like all incomers, he might find it hard to get help."

"He's importing his own. Got caravans for them and a mobile home for himself and his wife coming up by road tomorrow."

Hamish felt his fatigue leaving him. In order to finalize the deal, Peter would need to have signed the papers at the lawyers'.

"I'll be off in the morning early," he said. "I've got to see someone in Inverness."

"I'll put an alarm beside your bed," said Edie. "What time do you want breakfast?"

"About seven. I can make my own."

"Och, no, I'll be up and about. I've little else to do now the exercise classes have finished."

Hamish looked at her curiously. "Did Peter Hynd flirt with you?"

Her eyes grew dreamy. "Yes, he did. I felt

young again, excited, happy. And when he went away, I looked in the mirror and there again was just me, Edie Aubrey, middle-aged and plain. He had a knack of making every woman feel she was the one who was special to him. I thought I was his favourite, but now I've got over the madness I realize he was only playing around."

Hamish experienced a feeling of mounting excitement as he drove to Inverness, propelled southward by the Sutherland gale. One way or another, the investigation would now be over. With any luck he would find that Peter Hynd was alive and well. To think that any man in Drim was not only capable of impersonating a good-looking Englishman but also of forging his signature was ridiculous. And with any luck, Betty would turn out to have died from a heavy fall.

To his disappointment, the genial Mr. Brand was on holiday and he had to deal with his older, crusty partner, Mr. MacDougal. Mr. MacDougal listened impatiently to Hamish's request and then said, "I dealt with Mr. Hynd myself."

"That's great," said Hamish. "Did he tell you where he was staying?"

"Yes, he had come up from London. Jenny!" The pallid girl slouched in. "Bring

202

Mr. Hynd's address."

Hamish waited. A sea-gull perched on the window-ledge outside and looked in curiously through the grimy panes. Jenny came in and put a slip of paper in front of Hamish and he found himself looking down at the Vale of Health address. "This won't do," he said sharply. "That's the house he rents out."

"That's all we've got," said Mr. MacDougal. "Now, I'm very busy and I'm expecting a client." He stood up.

"One moment," said Hamish. "What did Peter Hynd look like?"

"Pleasant, upper class, fair hair, only stayed for as long as it took to sign the papers."

"May I take a copy of the papers? I would like to have the signature checked."

"Mr. Brand, who is a good fellow but too easygoing, told me he had faxed signatures to the bank in London already. Are you here on official business?"

"I'm just following up inquiries of my own."

"If you return with an official request from headquarters, then we will let you have the papers. Until then . . ."

When Hamish went into the outer office he asked Jenny, "Was the Peter Hynd who came to sign the final papers the one you had met before?"

"Why wouldn't it be?" she said rudely. "But I wouldn't be knowing. I got a ladder in my tights and ran out to get a new pair, and when I got back I heard he'd been in."

Hamish left the lawyers' in a bad mood. Surely it was silly to go on following this ridiculous hunch that Peter Hynd was dead. Still, to wrap it up neatly, it might be a good idea to go to Strathbane and get an official request to take those papers and have a handwriting expert check the signature. He decided to go over Blair's head. Blair would hate him for it, but then Blair hated him anyway.

To his surprise he was ushered into Mr. Daviot's office without having to wait, but the minute Mr. Daviot said solemnly, "Sit down, Macbeth," his heart sank. No "Hamish."

"I find to my surprise," said Mr. Daviot, "that you have chosen to take your holidays in Drim, of all places. My wife called on Priscilla with details of a house for sale and Priscilla told her that you appeared to have no interest in settling down."

Although Hamish was used to the Highland bush telegraph, he was always amazed at its speed. Harry Baxter, he thought.

Harry would tell the other fishermen in Lochdubh and the word would speed up to Tommel Castle Hotel.

"If we could put my personal life on one side," said Hamish. He explained his reasons for staying in Drim, his reasons for suspecting both the absence of Peter Hynd and the death of Betty Baxter. He ended up with his request to get the papers from the lawyers in Inverness.

The superintendent leaned back in his chair and surveyed the tall, gangling sergeant. He had tolerated his wife's social ambitions while privately thinking Priscilla much too good for Macbeth. Hamish had proved a clever if unorthodox policeman in the past, but Mr. Daviot thought he was hellbent on this wild-goose chase in order to stay away from Priscilla. What man in his right mind with a gorgeous fiancée like Priscilla Halburton-Smythe would choose to spend his holidays in a place like Drim? It showed a dangerous instability. Mr. Daviot preferred the plodding, obsequious type of policeman, which was why Blair, despite all his gaffes, had never been reduced to the ranks. Also, Mr. Daviot was a proud member of the Freemasons, as was Blair, and he remembered that Hamish had refused an invitation to join.

"I cannot control what you choose to do on your holidays, Macbeth," he said, "except to point out to you that you will get no help from me in this non-case. Peter Hynd, wherever he is, has sold his house and signed the papers. Betty Baxter had an unfortunate accident. That is that. I would like to suggest to you that you return to Lochdubh and pay more attention to Priscilla, but your private life is no concern of mine."

"Exactly," put in Hamish, turning red with annoyance.

"Do not waste valuable police time again, Macbeth. You may go."

Hamish left the room, walking as stiffly as an outraged cat.

As he drove out of Strathbane, he felt miserable and guilty about Priscilla. And yet he had no reason to feel guilty. She had brought it on herself.

But instead of turning off on the road that led to Drim, he went on to Lochdubh. As he drove along the waterfront he could feel curious eyes following his progress. "There goes the mad and fickle Hamish Macbeth, who prefers to spend his holidays in a place like Drim," they seemed to be saying.

There was a new receptionist at the Tommel Castle Hotel, a plain, middle-aged woman. "Where's Sophy?" he asked.

"If you mean Miss Bisset, she just walked out. I was working over at Cnothan and Mr. Johnston offered me the job if I could come immediately, so I did."

"Where is Miss Halburton-Smythe?"

"In the gift shop."

Hamish walked over to the gift shop. Priscilla was kneeling on the floor, unpacking a box of china. She looked up and saw him and her face hardened. "How are the sunny shores of Drim?" she asked.

"You wouldn't come on holiday with me," said Hamish. "I chust have to make my own amusement and that's trying to find out what happened to Peter Hynd."

She stood up and smoothed down her skirt. "While making a fool of me in the process?"

"What do you mean?"

"Everyone in the village now knows that the oh-so loving Hamish prefers to spend his holidays in a village a mere stone's throw away rather than be near me."

"And did you tell all these nosy folk you preferred to work rather than spend any time with me? Don't blame me for your fear o' intimacy, Priscilla."

"Don't be stupid."

"Then come to bed wi' me . . . now."

"I happen to be very busy."

"Spoken like a woman in love. Och, this is hopeless . . . absolutely hopeless." Hamish stormed out. He hurt so badly, he wondered bleakly if he was going to have ulcers.

All he had left in life was this mad case. And he would solve it even if it meant taking the whole village of Drim apart!

He stopped off at the police station to get extra clothes and make sure he really had switched everything off. The new cooker gleamed in the dark corner. He gave it a savage kick. And then the bell at the front door sounded. He had an impulse to let it go on ringing. After all, there was that notice on the door telling people that all inquiries were being handled from Cnothan. But curiosity beat sloth and he went and opened the door.

Mrs. Hendry, the schoolteacher's wife, stood there, her face blotched with tears.

"I saw the police car," she said in a choked voice. "I've got to speak to you, Mr. Macbeth."

CHAPTER 8

Good Lord, what is man! for as simple he
    looks,
Do but try to develop his hooks and his
    crooks,
With his depths and his shallows, his good
    and his evil,
All in all, he's a problem must puzzle the
    devil.

Robert Burns

"Come in," said Hamish. "Come ben to the
kitchen. It's not so formal as the police office."

He put an arm about her shaking shoulders and led her through.

She sat down at the kitchen table and put
her head in her hands. "I can't go on," she
said. "I'm so weary."

"He's been beating you, hasn't he?" asked
Hamish.

She nodded dumbly.

"And what about the children? How many have you got?"

"Two. Ann and Paul. Ann is twelve and Paul thirteen. I had them late. I had given up hope of having any children. He doesn't touch them . . . yet. But he runs the house like a military academy. They have very little freedom. Paul's starting to get into trouble, playing truant, mixing with a crowd of rough boys."

"Does your husband drink?"

"That's the trouble. Lately it's been getting worse. Dr. Jekyll turns into Mr. Hyde."

"Has he tried Alcoholics Anonymous?"

"I called him an alcoholic last night and this is what he did." She raised her sweater. There were red weals and bruises on her body.

"So you want to register an official complaint?"

She shook her head and began to cry again, so Hamish rose and put on the kettle and busied himself making tea until she was under control again.

"I can't," she said. "The next thing the social services would be round to take the children away."

Hamish looked at her bleakly. Ever since the famous Orkney case, where the social services and police had raided homes on the island at dawn and taken the children away to the mainland, mothers were terrified of having anything to do with them.

"So what can I do?" he asked.

"Perhaps you could have a word with him?"

"Perhaps I could. But the word I'll be having with him is not for the record books. I'll go back with you and wait for him. Keep the children away for an hour."

"You'll not hurt him?"

Hamish looked at her in grim amusement. "Only his ego," he said untruthfully. "You chust leave it to me."

He followed her car to Strathbane. She parked outside a trim bungalow. He waited, hearing her calling to the children. Then she reappeared and put the children in the car and drove off.

He waited a few moments and went up and rang the bell.

Mr. Hendry answered the door. Hamish immediately smelled whisky.

The schoolteacher blinked up at Hamish and said, "Oh, it's you. Come about the house?"

"If we could go inside . . ." Mr. Hendry stood back and walked through to the living-room. Hamish followed him.

"Do you want to look at it again?" asked Mr. Hendry.

"No, I want a good look at you. You've been beating your wife again."

"How dare —"

"Again. Now she hasn't laid a charge against you . . . yet. But I am convinced I can talk her into it."

"Prove it," sneered the schoolteacher.

"Oh, I could get her to a doctor to look at the bruises and weals on her body. You can either end up in court or we'll do it this way. You will pick up that phone and phone Alcoholics Anonymous and tell them you want to go to a meeting. You will neffer drink again."

Mr. Hendry's fist shot out but Hamish caught him by the wrist and twisted his arm up his back. "Stop it," shouted Mr. Hendry, "you're hurting me."

"Aye, just like you hurt your wife." Hamish ran his head into the wall and gave it a good bang. "Every time from now on that you hit her, I'll get to hear of it and come and hit you worse."

"This is police brutality, you fascist pig, you bourgeois lackey." Hamish listened in delight to these Stalinist phrases. Anyone of any other political persuasion would report him to headquarters. Only a drunk pertaining to the far left would think he was up against an establishment conspiracy.

He dragged the schoolteacher to the phone and stood over him. "Phone," he ordered, "or I'll kick your head in."

Mumbling and cursing, Mr. Hendry dialled the number. "When's the next meeting?" he snapped when a voice answered.

The voice at the other end said something. "My drinking's nothing to do with you," howled the schoolteacher.

Hamish took the phone away from him. "What he is trying to ask is where and when is the next AA meeting?"

"It's in the church in Market Square in half an hour," said the voice. "My name is Ron. Ask for me. I'm just leaving to go there."

"Right," Hamish banged down the phone.

Fifteen minutes later he thrust the still-cursing Mr. Hendry into the church-room, which was hung with slogans like EASY DOES IT and LIVE AND LET LIVE, reminding Hamish he wasn't doing much of either.

He did snatch up a pamphlet entitled "Help for the Family" and took it with him back to the Hendrys' house. He sat in the car and read it, parked outside. He noticed gloomily that it warned families that you could not force the drunk to get sober. All the family could do was to attend Al-Anon meetings for help for themselves.

Mrs. Hendry arrived with the children and he handed her the pamphlet. "He's at an AA meeting," said Hamish. "But you'd better read this and get some help yourself. And here is my phone number in Drim. If he lays a finger on you again, you're to phone me."

She thanked him but in a way that showed she was regretting the whole business already.

Feeling sad and slightly dirty, he wished he had taken the orthodox line and had got her to report her husband. He drove to a fish-and-chip shop and moodily ate fish and chips behind the driving wheel and then threw the remains to Strathbane's grimy scavenging sea-gulls.

Tomorrow was another day. He would doggedly stay in Drim. He thought Heather was right. Even if a murder had not taken place, he was convinced something pretty bad had happened there.

The next morning he went up to Jimmy Macleod's. Nancy was in the kitchen, grey roots poking through the dead black of her hair. "Oh, it's you," she said ungraciously.

"You'll find Jimmy out back in the shed."

"Did you see Peter Hynd leave the village?" asked Hamish.

She turned away from him and fiddled with a pot handle on the stove. "No. Why ask me? He came, he went. Like most incomers, that's all there is to it."

"Who put a brick through his window?"

"What is this? Folks are saying you are here on holiday?"

"Aye, but I'm curious all the same. Who threw the brick through his window?"

"Och, weans."

"What had children got against him?"

"Weans will be weans."

Hamish left and went out to the shed, where Jimmy was sharpening an axe.

"Grand day," said Hamish.

Jimmy scowled by way of reply.

Hamish leaned against the door-jamb. A pile of logs waited by a chopping block to be split. The air smelled pleasantly of pine. Outside, the day was still and clear, with white patches in the shade where the morning sun could not reach the frost. Up in the clear blue sky, two buzzards swirled and turned.

"Nice place, Drim," Hamish went on. "Full o' character. I haff often heard myself saying, 'Yes, Drim is the nicest place in the

Highlands. Good place for a holiday.' "

"Havers," said Jimmy sourly.

"Always the outstretched hand of welcome," said Hamish dreamily. "That's when the locals aren't heaving bricks through people's windows."

Jimmy stopped sharpening the axe. "I had nothing to do wi' that," he said.

"Who did?"

"Och, who knows or cares? We don't need strangers here."

"No? Aye, I suppose you all love each other that much. Neffer the hard word. Come off it, Jimmy. This place is a hotbed of spite."

"That's maybe the way an outsider sees it."

"Well, you'll be seeing a lot of me. Get used to it."

Hamish walked off. The one person who would speak to him was Heather. But he would need to wait until she came home from school.

He headed down to the manse. Annie Duncan answered the door. "I was expecting you," she said. "Come in."

Hamish looked at her appreciatively. She wore no makeup but her skin had a good colour and her long brown hair shone with health.

"Do you know why I am in Drim?" he asked.

"Oh, yes," she said calmly. "It's because of Betty Baxter's death. You think it might be murder."

"Yes, but I am also worried about the disappearance of Peter Hynd."

"But surely there is no mystery about that? He took his car and all his things."

"But no one saw him go. Did you?"

She shook her head and then said, "If he left in the middle of the night, no one would see him, would they? Everyone in this village sleeps like the dead."

"What about the brick that was thrown through Peter's window?"

"Oh, I can tell you about that. That was the men of the village led by that great big idiot, Jock Kennedy. They were trying to scare him out of the village and I suppose they succeeded, although it surprised me. Peter seemed to delight in getting people's backs up."

Hamish gave her a shrewd look. "You got wise to him?"

"Oh, yes. At first I was charmed like everyone else. But one had only to look at the way he tied these poor women up in knots. And yet he brought some life here. At least when everyone was at the exercise classes, there was a feeling of community. I have been speaking to Callum about that. I want to put on a Christmas show in the community hall. Some of the women do have good singing voices. A pantomime would be a good idea. I have already written off for a script. One can buy one of the traditional scripts and then just add in a few local jokes. You are staying with Edie? Yes, I have sent her a note inviting her and some of the other women to the manse tonight to discuss the project. It will give them an interest."

"I'll tell her. Now what about Betty Baxter? What do you think?"

"I think it probably was an accident," she said cautiously. "Betty was even heavier than she looked, I think. She slipped on the ice last winter and came down so heavily that she broke her hip."

"But why do you think after receiving a phone call would she get so excited, get her high heels on, get her hair bleached, and go out to walk on the beach?"

Annie shook her head. "It is strange. Yet have you thought all the same that there might not be a mystery?"

"I'll believe that when I see Peter Hynd in the flesh again."

"You could ask the new owner of his cottage. He's turned up with his wife and a squad of Geordie builders. Surely he saw Peter at some time during the negotiations."

"Good idea," said Hamish.

He left the manse and made his way to the cottage, hearing before it came in sight the unaccustomed sounds of busy activity. It was then that it struck him that Drim was normally a very quiet village. In Lochdubh, people stood chatting on the waterfront and calling to each other over garden fences. The air was always full of the sound of the boats chugging along the loch and the lap of waves on the shore.

As he approached the cottage, he saw that there was a mobile home parked at the side and two caravans in the garden in front. The corrugated-iron roof was being taken off. A stocky man came out of the mobile home and stopped when he saw Hamish approach.

Hamish held out his hand. "Welcome to the Highlands." The man shook the offered hand, a look of surprise on his face. "A welcome makes a nice change," he said. He had thinning hair, very black eyes, and a flat face and thin mouth. "My name's Apple," he said. "Fred Apple."

"I am a police sergeant from Lochdubh," said Hamish, "but I am here on holiday."

"I should have known you weren't from this neck of the woods," said Mr. Apple. "But I suppose once people here get to know us, they'll be friendly enough." The perpetual hopeful cry of the incomer, thought Hamish.

"I am interested in the whereabouts of the previous owner," said Hamish, "Did you meet him?"

Mr. Apple shook his head. "All done through my lawyers and his and the estate agent."

"May I see the deeds to the house?"

"They are down in Newcastle. I'll bring them up next week. Why?"

"I just wanted to check Mr. Hynd's signature. What do you plan to do here?"

Mr. Apple twisted round and waved an expansive arm. "Getting a decent roof on. He left a stack of good tiles. Then that field out back is a bit of a swamp. I want the men to drain it so that I can extend the house. I've always wanted the simple life. Get this place ready for retirement. The first thing they're going to do after the roof is to get the drains finished and put in a toilet and get that kitchen extension finished. Oh, and they'll raise the roof so we'll be able to have two bedrooms up there that you can stand up in."

"It'll be grand," said Hamish.

Mr. Apple looked at him curiously. "Is there more to your stay in Drim than just a holiday? I mean, I hear a woman was found dead on the beach."

"Well, there is," said Hamish. "Look, as an incomer, you could be of help to me. This Peter Hynd was philandering. See if you can hear any little snippets of gossip that might be of use and pass them on."

"Will do. But I'll be surprised if any of this lot talks to me."

He went back to Edie's and asked if there was any hope of a cup of tea. "I'll put the kettle on right away," said Edie. "It's nice to have a man to look after again."

"I've not been quite straight with you," said Hamish, sitting down at the kitchen table. "I am not really here on holiday. I cannot get Betty's death out of my mind or the way Peter Hynd left just like that. And why would Peter leave a note and his key with Jock Kennedy, of all people? I gather it was Jock who was the leader of the men who threw a brick through Peter's window."

"Oh, don't stir it all up again." Edie looked flushed and distressed. "We've been all settling down again. The atmosphere in Drim just before he left was dreadful, the men angry and the women at each other's throats."

"But if there has been a crime, then justice should be done," said Hamish quietly. "Now, a delicate question. Was it just flirting with Peter, or did any of the women go further than that? I found a blonde hairpin in Peter's bedroom, and that would point to Betty Baxter."

"Her!" Old jealousy flashed behind Edie's glasses. "A gentleman like Peter and that coarse quean! It doesn't bear thinking of. I . . . I don't think any of them went too far. Look at us all," said Edie sadly. "Oh, we all thought we looked like Sophia Loren while he was here, but once he went we were all reduced, diminished to a group of silly women who had temporarily lost their heads. Please just leave it alone. We're all going to the manse tonight to discuss the idea of putting on a pantomime. It's a good idea of Annie Duncan's. It'll draw us together."

Hamish accepted a cup of tea and looked at her sympathetically. "I'll be as discreet as I can. And if I've found out nothing by the end of my holiday, I'll leave it alone."

"I would have thought," said Edie, sitting down opposite him, "that you would have wanted to spend some time with Miss

Halburton-Smythe."

"Priscilla understands my interest in this case," said Hamish curtly.

He quickly changed the subject and asked her about the pantomime and Edie prattled away happily.

Hamish finished his tea and strolled down to the store, where Ailsa stood behind the counter. "Jock about?" asked Hamish.

Ailsa shook her fiery head. "Gone fishing."

"Then I might take out the rod and join him. Up on the Drim, is he?"

"Probably," said Ailsa.

"What do you think happened to Peter Hynd?" asked Hamish.

"I think he left because of the people in this village."

"You mean the men?"

"No, those silly bitches of women, slavering around him every step he took. He used to say to me, 'Ailsa,' he'd say, 'if it weren't for you, I would go mad.' "

Hamish looked at her, startled. "You're a good mimic, Ailsa," he said. "Just now, I could have sworn it was Peter himself talking."

"I was always good at the voices," she said.

"Do you think he'll come back?"

"Peter?" She leaned her elbows on the

counter and her blue eyes looked past him and through the glass doors of the shop to the black loch. "I sometimes think he will." In that moment, Hamish was sure she had forgotten he was there. "Sometimes, I think I'll look up and he'll just stroll into the shop and say, 'Hullo, Ailsa,' and he'll smile at me in that way he had." There was a short silence and then her eyes focused once more on Hamish Macbeth and her face hardened.

"Are you going to buy anything or not?" she demanded.

Hamish bought a bottle of lemonade and a Cornish pasty and took them outside to drink and eat. He was beginning to wish he had appreciated Priscilla's sensible cooking more than he had done. Junk food was all very well for a treat, but it was getting to be a constant diet. He had a longing to run over to Lochdubh and discuss the casc with Priscilla, but he knocked that idea out of his head. He must concentrate his whole mind on this case. Priscilla was no longer his Watson. He looked up and saw the slight figure of Heather moving homewards. He threw the remains of his lunch in the litter-bin outside the shop and hurried to catch up with her.

An official voice nagged in his brain that he should not be interviewing a minor without her parent being present, but he shrugged it away. He was on holiday and having a friendly chat.

"How are you doing, Heather?" he asked.

"Verra well, considering the circumstances."

"Those being?"

"One dead mother."

"Oh."

"Now if you don't mind, Mr. Macbeth, I have to get Da's tea ready."

"Stay a bit, Heather. Do you still think Peter Hynd was murdered?"

Those odd grey eyes looked up into Hamish's hazel ones and then dropped. "I think I made a mistake," said Heather. "I think I saw my own mother's death."

"Which was an accident?"

"Which was an accident," said Heather firmly.

She turned and scampered away from him. Hamish watched her go. Everything seemed to lead to a brick wall. Once again he wondered what Priscilla would make of Heather. He had a sudden longing to see her. He needed her mind, or so he persuaded himself.

He went back to Edie's and got in the police Land Rover. Now that he was actually going to see her, now that he was soaring up and out of Drim, he felt excited and impatient. He longed to put on the police siren, not to clear the way, for there was nothing else on the road, but for the sheer exhilaration of the sound.

When he drove up to the hotel, Priscilla was standing outside, saying farewell to a party of guests. She was wearing a black business suit with a white blouse. He was suddenly conscious of his baggy trousers and the frayed collar of his shirt. She seemed to belong to another world.

She saw him and half raised a hand in acknowledgement of his presence. He waited patiently until the guests had gone and then she turned towards him. "Hamish?"

"This is silly," he said. "No!" he added quickly, holding up his hand. "You're about to say that yes, it's silly of me to be spending my holidays in Drim and we'll get into a pointless, hurting argument, and I need help."

Her face softened. "I gather from Mrs. Daviot that you're not the flavour of the month. Come inside and tell me all about it."

He followed her into the office. "Where's Johnston?"

"Day off," said Priscilla. She shut the door. "Now tell me what's been going on."

He sat down in a chair by the window and stretched out his long legs. He outlined the few facts he had, about how he could not understand Heather, about how the atmosphere of Drim distorted everything, about how, on the face of it, it seemed as if Peter Hynd were indeed alive and had sold his house. He ended up by asking, "What did you think of him?"

"Do you know," said Priscilla, "if you had told me that Peter Hynd was a murderer, I would not have been surprised. He had great charm, but there was something ruthless and manipulative about him. I think if his vanity was wounded, he could turn vicious."

"But a man like that could be a murderee," Hamish pointed out. "Cruelty and viciousness create cruelty and viciousness. I feel like chucking the whole thing and returning to Lochdubh, but there's something there, I know there is."

A silence hung between them. Then Hamish said, "If only it were possible for you to have a wee word with Heather."

"Wee Heather appears to regard you as her property," said Priscilla. "If you remember, she did not want me to come with you that evening." She flushed slightly and again there was an awkward silence as both remembered the evening of love that never was.

"I could, though," said Priscilla after a few moments, "go back with you, if you would like. Things are quiet here."

"You could stay at Edie's with me, chust for a few days." Hamish brightened. He kept seeing that large double bed in Edie's spare room.

But that hope was dashed when Priscilla said, "I suppose Edie has another spare room."

"I suppose she has," said Hamish sulkily. "Why?"

"This is the Highlands of Scotland. We are not married."

"Oh." He realized the truth of what she said and reminded himself firmly that he had only come to get her help on the case.

The truth of what Priscilla had said was borne out when later that day they both arrived at Edie's. "To be sure, I am honoured you want to stay here," fluttered Edie, "but I've only got the little room at the end of the corridor. It's not as if you can share the same room."

"Then Priscilla can have my room and I'll take the wee one," said Hamish. "Don't worry, I'm used to roughing it."

Edie bridled. "There will be no need for

that, no need for that at all. Never let it be said that I cannot make a room comfortable."

Edie was brightening visibly by the minute. Not only had she the bonus of two paying guests out of season but she was flattered that Priscilla was staying. Certainly she did experience a certain pang of regret, for she had been looking forward to cosy evenings alone with Hamish Macbeth, but on the other hand, Priscilla's presence would give her a certain cachet.

Once the rooms had been changed and Priscilla had unpacked, Edie remembered she was due at the manse for the first meeting to arrange the pantomime. Priscilla, to Hamish's surprise, said she would like to go too, and the gratified Edie agreed to take her along. The efficient Priscilla then said she would go out shopping and make them a meal before they went to the manse. "What are you up to?" asked Hamish as they walked down to the shop together.

"It's a good way for me to meet the women of the village," said Priscilla. "No, you can't come. They'll talk more openly to me. We need a list of Peter Hynd's victims. I might be able to pick up some gossip."

"And what am I to do with myself?"

"You could try to have another talk with

Heather. Her father will be off at the fishing."

"All right, but there's something about that child that scares me."

Seated in a large dim drawing-room in the manse later that evening, Priscilla took stock of the assembled women. Hamish had given her thumb-nail sketches of the women who interested him most. Ailsa Kennedy was easily identified by her blue eyes and flaming red hair, Nancy Macleod by her black hair with the grey roots. Then there was the hairdresser, Alice MacQueen, sitting beside Edie. There were twelve other women there, but Hamish felt that Nancy, Alice, Edie, and Ailsa were the main characters, particularly Nancy and Ailsa. If murder had been done and done by a man, then it stood to reason it was a cuckolded man.

The minister's wife, Annie Duncan, had two spots of colour burning high on her cheeks. Priscilla and Edie had been the first to arrive and had heard from outside the manse, as they waited patiently for someone to answer the door, the faint sounds of what seemed to be a marital row.

Priscilla, after having registered that her presence seemed to be calmly accepted, settled down to admire the tact and efficiency of Annie, who was now discussing parts. The pantomime was to be *Puss in Boots.* For a number of women who had reportedly been at each other's throats only recently because of Peter Hynd, they appeared strangely docile now. There was no competition for parts. They passively let Annie choose who should do what. Annie herself was to be Dick Whittington, keeping to the British pantomime tradition of having a woman play Principal Boy. The choice of heroine was a surprise. Nancy Macleod was chosen, Nancy of the heavy body and greying hair. Various other parts were allotted, Annie making the suggestion that young Heather Baxter should be asked to play the cat because it might cheer her up. When the musical numbers were discussed and Nancy was urged to sing one of them, Priscilla realized why she had been chosen for the lead. She had a beautiful soprano voice, strong and clear as a bell, and as she sang she lost years, and the beautiful young girl she had once been showed through the tired middle-aged face. The evening finished amicably over tea and cakes. Priscilla felt let down. No rivalries. No undercurrents. Nothing to report to Hamish.

But as she walked away from the manse with Edie, her companion suddenly said bitterly, "Who does she think she is?"

"Who?" asked Priscilla.

"Herself. Lady Muck. Mrs. High and Mighty Annie Duncan. My singing voice is every bit as good as Nancy's. Nancy playing the lead! Nancy supposed to be a young girl with that lumpy figure o' hers. It's a crying shame. Not even discussed. Me, in the chorus. I've a good mind not to take part."

"That would be a shame," said Priscilla. "It'll all be good fun, you'll see."

"And did you see," went on Edie, unheeding, "the way Annie elected herself as Principal Boy. My legs are better'n hers any day."

In vain did Priscilla try to soothe her down. Edie would not be comforted. When they returned, Edie announced she was going to bed. "I'll look in Hamish's room and see if he's there," said Priscilla.

"Well, leave the bedroom door open," snapped Edie. "I'll have none of that in my house."

Priscilla pushed open the door of Hamish's room but it was empty. She returned to the kitchen just as Hamish came in.

"Did you see Heather?" asked Priscilla. "I'll make us some tea."

"No, I decided to drop in on Jock

Kennedy's. The back shop was full of men, drinking, but as Jock swore it was just a gathering of friends and no money changed hands, there was nothing I could do about it. It was all very boring, all the men carefully talking about sheep and fish. Then Ailsa came crashing in. It must have been a stormy meeting up at the manse."

"No, it seemed all very quiet. What did Ailsa say?"

"She started by cursing Annie Duncan for having chosen Nancy Macleod as the lead, with herself as the Principal Boy. Ailsa felt she herself should have got one of the main parts. She said that great lump Nancy would make a mockery of the whole thing. Up starts Jimmy Macleod and says his wife has the best voice between here and Inverness, and furthermore, *his* wife is a lady and not given to whoring around; and I had to stop Jock from hitting him, but Ailsa jeered, "That's what you think," and then suddenly everyone decided to go home. One minute the room was full of men, and the next they had all faded out into the night."

"Goodness, Hamish, if you had been at the manse, you would have thought them all the best of friends. It was only when we left that Edie began to complain like mad about Annie Duncan's high-handedness, and yet there was nothing high-handed in Annie's behaviour. They seemed to placidly accept all her suggestions."

"Well, as you know, there is always a sort of tradition about letting the minister's wife have her way."

"There's just one little thing." Priscilla hesitated.

"Go on," said Hamish morosely. "Anything'll help, we haven't got much."

"When Edie and I arrived at the manse, we heard the minister and his wife having a row."

"Could you hear what it was about?"

"No, couldn't make out the words. The walls are thick."

"And the reverend didn't join you ladies at any point?"

Priscilla shook her head.

"So where do we go from here?" asked Hamish.

"For a start, there's the first rehearsal tomorrow afternoon in the community hall. The scripts haven't arrived yet, but Annie's going to run through the musical numbers."

"You go," said Hamish, "and maybe I'll drop in. Perhaps we should pay a visit on Heather . . . both of us. I'd like to know what you make of her."

CHAPTER 9

Retired to their tea and scandal, according to their ancient custom.

William Congreve

Heather was singing to herself and scrubbing the kitchen floor when Priscilla and Hamish arrived the following morning. She looked up and saw Priscilla and primmed her lips in disapproval.

"We are on the telephone," she said, getting to her feet. "We don't like people chust dropping in. This is still a house of grief."

"Just a few more questions," said Hamish easily.

"Why?" demanded Heather, wiping soapy hands on her apron. "You're supposed to be here on holiday."

"I don't suppose you believe that any more than anyone else," said Hamish.

Heather's eyes slanted at Priscilla. "What's she doing here?"

"Manners!" said Hamish sharply.

Heather folded her arms. "It's my house and I can say what I like."

"I'll go outside and take a look around," said Priscilla quickly.

As soon as she had gone, Heather appeared to relax. "A coffee or a cup of tea, Mr. Macbeth?" she asked in housewifely tones.

"Nothing at the moment," said Hamish. "You're a bit hard on Priscilla, Heather. What's she ever done to you?"

"She's a woman," said Heather curtly. "Don't like women much. They're cruel."

"Well, there are some nice women around. Mrs. Duncan has been verra kind to you, surely."

"Oh, aye. She's the minister's wife and it's her duty to be nice to people. Do you know I am to play the part of the cat in the pantomime?"

"No," said Hamish, that being a piece of news Priscilla had failed to tell him. "Will you like that?"

She wrinkled her brow. "It might be fine." She curled her small hands into imitation paws and pretended to wash her face. "Aye, I reckon I could do that verra well."

"So," said Hamish, pulling out a chair and sitting down, "you go here and there about the village without anyone noticing you much. You must hear things. Do you know any woman who was . . . er . . . involved with Peter Hynd?"

Her eyes were suddenly like cold steel. "You mean who wass he screwing? My ain mither, for one."

"Heather, you're verra young. How can you know that?"

"Because I followed her up to his cottage one night," she said wearily. She sat down at the table opposite him and rested her small pointed chin on her hands.

"B-but how could you know?" asked Hamish, blushing a deep red.

"I heard them."

"But not *saw*. You might have been mistaken. You're only twelve."

She jerked her head towards the television set in the corner. "I see and hear it all on that."

Oh, the lost days of youth, thought Hamish bitterly. Aloud he said, "It must have been hard for you."

"Peter Hynd was an evil man," she said. "Really evil. I'm glad he's gone."

"But you no longer think he was killed?"

"That wass chust a fancy."

Hamish felt he should not be asking one so young the next question, but who else in this village was going to tell him? "Heather," he said, "do you know which of the others were sleeping with Peter Hynd?"

She held up a slim hand and ticked off the names on her fingers: "Nancy Macleod, Ailsa Kennedy, Alice MacQueen, and Edie Aubrey."

"I cannae believe that! Edie! Come on, Heather."

"The uglier they come, the harder they fall," said Heather. "Now, Da will be back from the fishing and I've got to get his dinner on. I will speak to you again, Mr. Macbeth."

"And I hope I'm strong enough to take it," said Hamish after he had rejoined Priscilla and repeated what Heather had said. "What do you make of her?"

"I think she is a remarkably strong and self-disciplined little girl who is delighted to run the house and have her father to herself," said Priscilla. "Of course, I may be wrong. It could all be a front. The child could be teetering on the edge of a nervous breakdown for all I know. But those women she listed! And her own mother. I can hardly believe it of Edie."

"There's one way to find out," Hamish pointed out. "I could ask Edie point-blank. All she has to do is to deny it."

"You know," said Priscilla, "we're barking up the wrong tree. Let's look at this another way around. Let's assume Peter Hynd was murdered and Betty Baxter was murdered. Who had the best motive? Why, the husband, Harry. Harry finds out Betty has been unfaithful to him. He murders Peter Hynd and gets rid of Peter's belongings. The place is full of peatbogs where stuff, including Peter's body and Peter's car, could be sunk without trace. The murder twists his brain further and so he calls Betty and somehow gets her to think he is Peter, don't ask me how, follows her down to the beach, and breaks her neck. He tells Heather to back him up on the frozen-cod story and she, being happy to have her mother out of the way, goes along with it."

"Except for one thing," Hamish pointed out. "Harry Baxter has a cast-iron alibi."

"*Does* he?" asked Priscilla eagerly. "We assume Betty was killed about seven in the morning. What if it were earlier? A post-mortem cannot tell the exact time of death. The fishing boats often come in around six."

"Thought about that. Harry Baxter went straight to the bar. The bar opens up for the fishermen."

Priscilla frowned. "Lochdubh is a close-knit community. Gossip from Drim filters over there. Harry would be pitied by his cronies. Say he did not go out fishing or say he did not go to the bar, would his friends cover up for him to get him out of trouble?"

Hamish's hazel eyes gleamed. "They might at that. They don't like Blair — who does? — and as they would think that poor old Harry would never do such a thing in a hundred years, they just could have decided to give him an alibi."

"There's Archie Maclean's wife," said Priscilla. "She waits on the harbour for the boats to come in. Which boat is Harry on again?"

"The *Silver Princess*. Archie's boat."

"Let's go to Lochdubh," urged Priscilla. "We can get some sandwiches for lunch at the hotel. I never realized before how inconvenient this bed-and-breakfast-only arrangement is. How do the poor holiday-makers fare when it's pouring wet?"

"Goodness knows," said Hamish. "I suppose they just drive around looking at wet sheep and eating in cafés until it's safe to return. Mrs. Wellington, the minister's wife in Lochdubh, she ran bed-and-breakfast for a wee while, and her guests had to be out of the house at nine in the morning whatever the weather and were ordered not to return until eight-thirty in the evening."

"Let's go to Lochdubh anyway. It'll be a relief to get out of here."

It was a crisp, cold day. Both felt it amazing that two such villages as Lochdubh and Drim could exist in the north of Scotland, two such vastly different villages. Lochdubh as usual was full of the sounds of life.

"Let's try Archie first," suggested Hamish.

Mrs. Maclean was scrubbing the kitchen counters. Not for her the easy road of plastic or laminated surface. She attacked the pine wood with a scrubbing brush with tremendous ferocity and looked up in disapproval when Hamish popped his head around the door. "I'm busy," she snapped.

Hamish strolled into the kitchen, with Priscilla after him. "Just a few questions," he said.

"You're not in uniform," said Mrs. Maclean, throwing the scrubbing brush in the bucket and rubbing her red hands dry on a towel that looked as if it had been starched.

"This is unofficial. Where's Archie? Asleep?"

"Drinking, as usual."

"We'll get round to him in a minute. Now, you go down to the harbour to see the boat come in, don't you?"

She put her hands on her hips. "And what if I do? That's no crime. Like to see my man come in safely."

"Aye, well. The day Betty Baxter over at Drim was killed, can you remember if Harry Baxter was out on the boat the night before?"

She turned away and took the brush out of the bucket and fell to scrubbing again. "I cannae remember one morning from another," she said.

"But that would be the morning the police came around asking the fishermen questions," said Priscilla. "And as Archie is skipper of the boat Harry was supposed to be on, they must have called here. Surely you remember that?"

"I tell you, I'm too busy," she said, scrubbing unabated. "They didnae see me. They asked Archie."

Hamish raised his eyes to heaven. "Come on, Priscilla," he said. "We'd better ask Archie."

He glanced back in the kitchen window as they walked through the garden. "She's on the phone already," he said. "Let's get to the bar fast."

The fishermen were divided into two groups, those who drank and those who did not drink at all, and the ones who drank could sink leg-fuls of the stuff, and so most of them were still there. As they came in,

Archie was just replacing the receiver on the phone on the bar.

"Hullo, Hamish," he said sheepishly. "What are you having?"

"Nothing at the moment. Too early. Archie, as your wife has just told you, we're checking up on Harry Baxter's alibi."

"And chust when did herself join the polis?" Archie jerked his head in Priscilla's direction. He looked uncomfortable, but then Archie always looked uncomfortable. The locals swore his wife boiled his clothes. His pullover was riding up somewhere about his midriff and was so felted, it looked like cloth.

"Don't get cheeky with me," said Hamish. "Come on, Archie, I'm going to keep after you and keep after you until I get at the truth."

"And I'm telling you Harry wass out on the boat, chust like I told thon great pudding, Blair."

"And I'm telling you that I'm not only going to ask your crew but the other fishermen and the women who wait for them and everyone else in Lochdubh, and then I'll have great pleasure in hauling you off to prison for impeding the police in their inquiries, bearing false witness, and downright lying."

"Och, Hamish, ye wouldna.' "

"That I would."

Archie looked wildly around and then picked up his drink. "Come ower in the corner."

They followed him over to a small rickety, beer-stained table in the corner and sat down.

"It iss like this," wheedled Archie, "we all heard how this foreigner was playing fast and loose wi' the wimmin o' Drim. Harry did show up for the fishing. It wass a bad night and we decided to go home early. We got into harbour about five, and Harry, he went straight home. Och, he had told us about his missus going a bit off her head and dying her hair and whatnot. When wee Heather phoned us and said it would be better to say her da wass in the bar, we thocht it was all right."

"Heather!"

"Herself said how her ma had been found dead on the beach wi' her neck broke in a fall. She says how it wass the accident but that the polis haeing the nasty minds might say her da pushed Betty. She wass crying hard, and if a wee bitty lassie thinks her da didnae do it, it iss surely all right to protect the man."

"I think we'd best be going back to have a

word with wee Heather," said Priscilla in a thin voice.

"Don't be too hard on the lassie," wheedled Archie. "Herself hass had a bad shock."

"And so have I," said Hamish grimly after he and Priscilla had had a brief lunch of sandwiches and coffee and were heading back to Drim. "Heather is beginning to appear quite the Lady Macbeth. Maybe she put her father up to it."

"And maybe she's just a frightened little girl doing her best to protect her father," said Priscilla. "I'll go over to the community hall when we get there and join the rehearsal. You had best see Heather on your own."

"I'll see Harry too," said Hamish. "There's no fishing tonight, so he'll be up and about by now. He must have gone straight home this morning."

As Hamish approached the Baxters' cottage, Heather was standing outside and he knew all at once that she was waiting for him and cursed the invention of the telephone. Of course Archie would have phoned her as soon as they had left the bar.

"Come in, Mr. Macbeth," she said formally. "Da's in the kitchen."

Hamish ducked his head and went inside.

"Now, Harry," he said, "this is the bad business. Don't you see how it looks?"

Harry Baxter was sitting with a mug of coffee between his gnarled hands. "I didnae know rightly what I wass doing, Hamish," he said. "Heather told me what she had done and it seemed safest to go along with it. But what does it matter? It's all over now. It wass the accident. Can't you see how bad it is for me, for Heather, for you to go over it and over it, keeping it green?"

"Tell me about the phone call Betty got," said Hamish.

"I heard her go to the phone. She chust said 'Yes' and 'No,' and then, 'I'll see you.' When she came back in, her face was all lit up. She said it was Edie. I lost ma rag and started to shout. When I woke up later, she had her hair all blonded up again. That's when I struck her. I said I knew that Peter Hynd had come back and had arranged to meet her. She paid me no heed. She said if I ever raised my hand to her again, she would leave me for good."

"You came straight back from the fishing. Did you go looking for her?" asked Hamish.

"No," he mumbled. "I wass that fed up, I chust went to my bed and went to sleep. The next thing I knew, the neighbours were round saying kids had found her body on the beach."

"It's no use me asking Heather to confirm your story," said Hamish wearily. "Look, answer this honestly. Did any of the locals see anything of Peter Hynd around the village the day your wife died or the day before?"

Harry shook his head. "I asked and asked," he said. "But no one's seen hide nor hair of the man since he left."

"And did anyone actually see him leave?"

Again Harry shook his head. "And I asked about that as well," he said. "God, I wanted more than anything in the world to make sure that wass the last o' him. He'd gone all right, but no one saw him leave."

Hamish felt as if his brain were full of cobwebs when he left. If he stood back from the case and considered the fact that Peter Hynd might just have packed up and left . . . There was all the evidence for that. He had put his house on the market before he had disappeared. Betty, having got a taste for extra-marital affairs, could have gone out to meet someone else, someone from the village, and she could have tripped and fallen onto the rocks. Hamish frowned. But she hadn't been carrying a handbag, nor had her hands been in her pockets, so why hadn't she put out her hands to save herself?

He should have reprimanded Heather, but somehow he could not bring himself to do so. He wished briefly he were a policeman like Blair and in Drim officially and he could harass the suspects without worrying about their feelings. Blair would have no difficulty, say, in approaching Edie and saying something tactful like "So ye let Hynd get his leg over?"

He sighed and went down to the community hall. To his surprise when he entered, he saw the small figure of Heather. She must have cut across the fields in her usual quick and silent way to get ahead of him. A massive woman was sitting at the piano. Nancy began to sing. Like Priscilla, Hamish was amazed at the purity and beauty of her voice. Annie Duncan joined her and began to sing as well, her voice deeper than Nancy's. A spattering of applause from the women greeted the end of the song and Hamish, looking around, could see no sign of the bitter animosity that must lurk under each bosom. But then, that was the Highland way.

He sat down next to Priscilla. "Going well?" he asked.

"On the face of it," said Priscilla. "Annie got the script this morning and went over to Strathbane and got it photocopied. She's a good organizer. They might not like her choices, but it's my belief they'll all knuckle down and do what she says. Oh, one piece of gossip from the woman at the piano, Mrs. Denby, who cleans the manse. She says that the minister is dead set against theatricals and told Annie she was to drop the idea and Annie told him she would do no such thing. Mrs. Denby says she's never heard them having rows before, but they're having them almost every day now. Seems like Callum Duncan is the kind who likes his wife to be a sort of glorified servant, and 'Yes, sir, no sir,' and suddenly Annie's having none of it and is rebelling at the slighest thing, telling him to make his own bloody tea when he summons her to the study and tells her to fetch him a cup, things like that."

"That would only be of use if the minister murdered his wife," said Hamish. Heather was now up on the stage getting her instructions, listening intently, holding the script, her eyes shining.

"And the villagers say Heather hasn't shed a tear," went on Priscilla. "Something wrong there, Hamish. It's unnatural. I wish she would crack and break down and cry."

"I've never seen a child further from tears," said Hamish cynically.

Annie Duncan's voice could be heard suggesting they all now read their parts in the first act. "And just here, after the first scene," she said to Nancy, "you exit left where the steps go down to the dressing-rooms."

"Dressing-rooms?" queried Hamish. "In a community hall?"

"Oh, this place is quite well-appointed," said Priscilla. "One of those projects built quite recently by the Highland and Islands Development Board. There's even a star dressing-room. Wonder who's got that. Nancy, probably."

In the first act, Nancy, the alderman's daughter dreaming of the famous man who would one day marry her, sang an Andrew Lloyd Webber song. "Heavy royalties, that," murmured Hamish.

"Why?" asked Priscilla. "Do you think they're going to tell him, or that he'll ever find out?"

The chorus of women backed Nancy and then exited right, leaving her alone on the stage. At the end of the song Nancy sailed off the stage with all the aplomb of a diva, but before the scene could switch to Dick Whittington and his cat, there was a scream from off-stage and the sound of a heavy fall.

Hamish ran forward, leaped on the stage, and ran to the exit stairs where Nancy had gone down. Nancy was lying at the foot of the stairs, her face contorted with pain.

"Don't move," he called.

He went down and crouched over her. "Easy now. Where does it hurt?"

"All over," groaned Nancy.

"Here." He put an arm behind her shoulders and eased her up. "Move your arms." She cautiously did as she was told. "Now your legs, right and then left. That seems all right. Now, I'm going to help you up. Take it easy."

He lifted Nancy to her feet. "There, you're all right," he said with relief, "although I'm sure you'll have some bruises. What happened?"

"Something seemed to catch at my ankles," she said, bewildered, "and over I went."

"Come to the dressing-room and sit down," said Annie Duncan. "I've got a flask of tea. Ailsa, tell the rest we'll leave the rehearsals until the same time tomorrow."

"Right," said Ailsa, and Hamish saw her give a mock Gestapo salute behind Annie's back.

Priscilla, ever efficient, had appeared to help Nancy along to the dressing-room. The rest of the women disappeared and Hamish was left alone.

He crawled up the stairs on his hands and knees, examining every inch. No sign of any string having been tied across the stairs, nothing on the thin iron banister.

He went back down and stood to one side of the staircase and reached through. Yes, someone could have stood here easily and caught at Nancy's ankles. The chorus had gone off to the right. But one of the women could easily have nipped round under the stage and waited for Nancy to come down. Another accident? Spite? Had Nancy broken a leg, she would have been out of the production. He felt a sudden fury against the inhabitants of Drim. And then he saw it, lying in a dark corner. It was one of those old-fashioned window-poles with a hook at the end for reaching the catch of windows high up in a church or a hall.

Now that, he thought, thrust through the banisters as Nancy came down, could have sent her flying. He longed for it to be an official case. He would even have gladly put up with Blair in order to get a forensic team to go over that pole for fingerprints.

Priscilla appeared behind him, making him jump. "You don't think it was an accident, do you, Hamish?"

"Maybe. I think someone could have taken this pole and thrust it across the staircase just as Nancy came down. Who could it be?"

"Well, Nancy was alone on the stage apart from the pianist. Let's go back and ask Edie if she saw anything."

Edie, when appealed to, looked startled. The women, she said, had sort of bunched together off the stage. Some had remained standing at the top at the right, watching Nancy, but she couldn't be sure which ones. She herself had gone down to the large dressing-room shared by the chorus to put on some powder. Oh, and she had seen Jock Kennedy.

"And what was himself doing there?" asked Hamish.

"Annie had asked him to call in to help with the props. We haven't any scenery yet, but she wanted to go over the lighting and stuff with him."

"But he wasn't anywhere in the hall," exclaimed Priscilla. "I would have noticed!"

"There's a door at the back which leads under the stage," said Edie. "Anyone can come in that way."

Anyone, thought Hamish bleakly, anyone in the whole of Drim, including Nancy's husband. But it would have to be someone who had been *there,* who knew that Nancy would come down the stairs at exactly that time.

"What's all this anyway?" demanded Edie, a trifle huffily. "It was just another accident."

"Another one too many," said Hamish grimly.

He surveyed Edie. Who, looking at her, could imagine her having an affair with a young man? Had Heather made up that list of names to throw him off the scent?

"Edie," he began, "how close were you to Peter?"

Her face took on a guarded look. "We were friends," she said cautiously. "He said I was the only one he could talk to."

"And did you have an affair with him?"

Edie blushed painfully and her eyes filled with tears.

"Don't be embarrassed," said Priscilla. "Everyone has affairs these days." Hamish glared at her. Except you, he thought.

Edie nodded wordlessly. There was an awkward silence.

"I don't want to upset you," said Hamish gently, "but you must have known you weren't the only one."

"I thought I was," said Edie piteously. "He let me think I was. 'Don't come to the cottage unless I ask you to, Edie,' he said, but then he stopped inviting me and I . . . I got all dressed up one night. I couldn't believe he had gone off me, after all that he had said, after all we had done." She choked and then regained some composure. "I should have knocked. Like the fool I was, I thought I would surprise him. I'd been into Strathbane that day to buy a bottle of champagne and I had it under my arm. I opened the door, it wasn't locked, and went in. The ladder was there, up to the bedroom. I climbed up. And then I heard them. Betty Baxter and Peter. I couldn't believe it. I went on up. Well, they were fortunately too busy to see me. I crawled back down the ladder and left as quietly as I could. I was so wretched I felt like killing myself. Betty Baxter! If it had been someone like her" — she jerked a thumb at Priscilla — "I could have borne it better."

"But when I asked you about Peter, you were quite . . . er . . . kindly about him," said Hamish.

"When he left," said Edie, "and the days passed and he did not return, I built up a dream about him. I put that awful night out of my head. I talked myself into thinking I was the only one. I remembered all the nice things he had said to me. It was easy with him not being here. It's better to dream, it's safer to dream."

Hamish looked at her bleakly, thinking in that moment that he had been happier when he had only dreamed about Priscilla, for now that she was engaged to him, however unofficially, she seemed more remote than she had ever been.

"And was there anyone else that you know of?" asked Priscilla quietly.

"Not for sure, but jealousy makes the senses awfully sharp. I began to notice that Ailsa was beginning to look triumphant and that Betty's eyes were often red with crying."

"But how could Ailsa get a chance to have an affair?" asked Hamish. "Aren't she and Jock together all day?"

"When Jock has his cronies in for a drink in the evening," said Edie, "Ailsa often goes out to visit some of the women in the village. Alice MacQueen was her friend for a while, but that is finished. Oh, they still talk, but in a funny sort of cold way."

"Did you ever confront Peter with the fact that you knew he had been sleeping with Betty Baxter?" asked Priscilla.

Edie shook her head. "I couldn't. I couldn't bear to hear him admit it. What's the point in all this? He's gone, and he's never coming back."

"Why do you say that?" asked Hamish quickly. "Do *you* think he's dead?"

"Dead?" Her surprise appeared totally genuine. "Why would Peter be dead?"

"Why not?" put in Priscilla. "Don't you think with the way he's been going on, that some irate husband might not have bumped him off and that's why no one saw him leave?"

"Oh, no." Edie shook her head. "We may have our difficulties in Drim, but there's no one here who would do a thing like that."

"But Drim had never been subjected to such as Peter Hynd before," said Hamish bitterly. "Sorry to have upset you, Edie. Come along, Priscilla. We have a call to make."

"Where are we going?" asked Priscilla when they were outside.

"I think we'll try Alice MacQueen, and then I'll tackle Jock Kennedy and Jimmy Macleod on my own."

"I hate this," said Priscilla as they walked side by side to the hairdresser's.

"Then don't come." Hamish slanted a look at her. "All this unbridled passion must be foreign to you."

"Don't get at me, Hamish."

"Maybe you'd best leave Alice to me. Why not visit Annie Duncan yourself, Priscilla?

She must have known what was going on. Goodness knows, she was there when I tried to warn the minister."

"Yes, sir," said Priscilla and turned and walked off in the direction of the manse. He stood for a moment watching her go, debating whether to run after her and give her a good shake. Then he shrugged and went on his way.

Alice MacQueen opened the door to him. "I was just about to watch a show on the telly," she said defensively.

"I've come about Peter Hynd."

She backed away from him, her hand to her mouth. "So he's been found," she said.

Hamish followed her in. "What do you mean by that?"

She sat down in one of the hairdressing chairs. "I meant, has he come back?"

"Now why do I think that wass not what you meant at all?" said Hamish, his voice suddenly sibilant. "What would you be saying if I told you that the body of Peter Hynd had been found in a peatbog?"

"He can't be dead," wailed Alice.

Hamish relented. "No, he hasn't been found."

She goggled at him and then said furiously, "Why are you playing nasty games with me?"

Hamish sat down. "I want to get at the truth, Alice. Something's wrong in Drim. Peter Hynd leaves and no one sees him go. Betty Baxter meets her death on the beach after she went out to meet someone, and someone tried to injure Nancy Macleod today."

"That was the accident," panted Alice. "She's too heavy and she looks ridiculous playing the lead."

"Well, let's begin at the beginning. Let's have a talk about Peter Hynd. Did you haff the affair wi' him?"

She shook her head.

"You're sure about that?"

Her eyes flashed. "It was nothing like that. It was innocent. A boy-and-girl thing."

How old was Alice? wondered Hamish. There was a puffiness under the eyes and little wrinkles radiated out from around her mouth. Fifty-five?

"Describe this boy-and-girl thing."

"You wouldn't understand," she said, suddenly weary. "We talked a lot and went for walks on the moors. He . . . held my hand. He said he could talk to me. He said I wasn't like the other women. He said . . . he said he had never met anyone like me. And then Betty Baxter with her great gross body took him away."

"You mean she had an affair wi' him?"

"She took away his innocence," said Alice, all mad logic. "But herself always was a slut. It's Ailsa I can't forgive."

"Ailsa?"

"We were friends. I began to guess what was happening when Jock asked me one day, casual-like, if the video had been any good. I said, 'What video?' 'Oh,' he says, 'the one you were watching last night with Ailsa.' I realized I had to cover for her for some reason, so I said it was great. I waited until I saw Ailsa next and asked her what it was about. She came home with me. She said she had a great secret to tell me. She was all excited. I should have known then what it was, but she was so excited and happy, I thought maybe she'd had a win on the football pools. She told me she had been with Peter . . . in bed. I was hurt and horrified. I said I had told her about my romance with Peter and how could she do such a thing? 'Romance,' she jeered. 'What romance? Wandering about the heather holding hands? Grow up, Alice,' she said. 'I'm a real woman to him.'

"I told her he would betray her as he had betrayed me, but she went on laughing and laughing. And when he went away, she wanted to be friends again, and what could I do? You know what a small village is like, it's not like the city. You have to get on with people. But Ailsa and I, we can't be friends anymore like in the old days. In fact, there were the five of us, Betty, Nancy, Ailsa, Edie, and me. We were close. We had a lot of laughs. When Peter Hynd first came, well, that was a laugh, too. They'd come to get their hair done and Edie's exercise classes were a big success and we competed with each other to see who had talked to Peter last, but it was all friendly, all joshing. Then it all turned sour. I don't really think I can go on living here."

Not for the first time did Hamish Macbeth curse Peter Hynd under his breath. "Alice, did Peter know that you were all the best of friends?"

"Oh, yes. I used to tell him how lucky I was."

And Peter promptly set out to turn one against the other, thought Hamish. He felt suddenly tired. If only Peter Hynd were alive and well so that he could punch him on the nose!

Priscilla wondered, as she sat in the manse, if Hamish Macbeth would one day float away on a sea of tea and coffee. Every house one went into in the Highlands, one was offered some form of refreshment, and to refuse would be tantamount to saying that one did not like one's host. She was glad the minister had left them alone. For some reason she could not fathom, Priscilla had found herself disliking him intensely. When the minister left, Priscilla felt the rather chilly air of the manse parlour lightening perceptibly. "We'll have some more coal on that fire for a start," said Annie, rising and suiting the action to the words. "I hate the way Callum rations it. I sometimes wish we had one of those new council houses, the ones with the central heating."

Priscilla studied her hostess. She looked much younger than her years, she must be at least fifty, but with her long hair worn down her back and her well-spaced features she could easily have been taken for a woman in her thirties, and early thirties at that. Her figure was slim and well-shaped. Her dress was surprisingly Bohemian for a minister's wife, Bohemian in a sort of old-fashioned way. She wore a white "peasant" blouse with patchwork skirt and fringed calfskin boots.

"Do you think the pantomime will be a success?" asked Priscilla.

"Oh, I think so. It doesn't look much like it at the moment. I'm borrowing costumes from the theatre in Strathbane. Once they see the costumes, they'll get excited. Fortunately the girl who played the lead in the same pantomime in Strathbane last Christmas was on the heavy side, so there shouldn't be that much of an alteration to get Nancy into it."

"Why Nancy?" asked Priscilla curiously. "She's hardly sweet sixteen."

"She's got a beautiful voice and that's all that matters. People get irritated when the lead has a tinny voice. Look at those huge opera singers. No one bothers about their size when they start to sing."

"But," said Priscilla tentatively, "your choice of Nancy seems to have caused a certain amount of animosity. I mean, someone could have caused her to fall down those stairs."

"Oh, believe me, I have survived here by never paying any attention to the squabbles of the village women."

And in that sentence, thought Priscilla, Annie had betrayed that she looked on the women of the village as some strange tribe of aborigines whose jealousies and feuds had nothing to do with a civilized being. How could she have lived here so long, marvelled Priscilla, and maintained that attitude? Priscilla knew most of the women in Lochdubh and liked quite a few of them.

"Did you know this Peter Hynd who started all the trouble?" asked Priscilla.

"Yes, he was a frequent visitor to the manse. We both liked him."

"He seems to have been a very manipulative young man, setting one woman against the other, and quite deliberately, too."

Annie looked amused. "Your fiancé is cursed with a Highland imagination. Your Highlander is an incurable romantic. Peter caused a bit of a flutter, that was all."

"I think there was more to it than that. No, no more tea for me, thank you. I gather he had affairs with at least five of them — Betty Baxter, Ailsa Kennedy, Nancy Macleod, Edie Aubrey, and Alice MacQueen."

"Now, I really must take you to task, Priscilla. I may call you Priscilla, may I not? No one is formal these days. You have been listening to wild gossip and perhaps stupid bragging on the part of these women. Do you know who you are dealing with here? They believe in fairies in this village. Nancy Macleod leaves a saucer of milk outside the door every night for the fairies."

"And do they drink it?" asked Priscilla,

momentarily diverted.

"They don't, but a fat hedgehog does."

Priscilla returned to the subject of Peter Hynd but could not seem to get anywhere. In fact, the minister's wife's manner grew somewhat supercilious, as if Annie Duncan had decided that Priscilla Halburton-Smythe was a sort of peasant in couture clothing. Perhaps it was the suddenly dying fire — the coal was poor quality — but a frost seemed to be settling on the room. When Priscilla stood up to leave, Annie barely managed to disguise her relief.

"One of the troubles about being a minister's wife," said Annie brightly, as she showed Priscilla out, "is that people *will* drop in unannounced. Do phone next time to say you are coming."

"And so I left with a flea in both ears," said Priscilla to Hamish when she arrived back at Edie's. "Where is Edie?"

"Gone to bed."

"And how did you get on, Hamish?"

"It was pretty awful," said Hamish. "Before Peter came to this village, Nancy, Betty, Edie, Alice, and Ailsa were all the best of friends. Peter knew that and set out, I am convinced, quite deliberately, to put one against the other. Alice swears she didn't have an affair with Peter. A boy-girl ro-

265

mance, she said, poor soul. Och, I'm tired." He stood up and walked round the kitchen table and put his hands on her shoulders, feeling them stiffen at his touch. He bent down and placed a swift kiss on her cheek. "I'll need to tackle Jock Kennedy tomorrow," he said.

"Next to Harry Baxter, he must be prime suspect," said Priscilla. "Peter beats him in a fight in a particularly nasty way and Peter lays his wife. It's funny, usually you can't cough in a Highland village during the night without everyone next day asking you if you've caught a cold, and yet Peter went off, car, papers, bags, and baggage without anyone hearing a thing."

"There are times of the night when no one notices anything," said Hamish, thinking of his own poaching forays. "From about three in the morning until five, everything's as dead as the grave. Are you coming?"

"I'll just wash up these cups for Edie," said Priscilla evasively. Hamish looked down sadly at the back of her smooth bright head. He'd tell her tomorrow that the engagement that never was, or whatever it had been, was at an end. He could not spend another day with all the unspoken words lying between them.

CHAPTER 10

The expense of spirit in a waste of shame
Is lust in action; and till action, lust
Is perjur'd, murderous, bloody, full of
  blame,
Savage, extreme, rude, cruel, not to trust.
                          William Shakespeare

Hamish could feel the tension and anxiety in the air as he pushed open the door of Jock's shop in the morning. Customers had been chatting before he went in — he had heard them through the open door — but as soon as he walked in, all fell silent, and then, one by one, they gradually faded away in that Highland style of departing without apparently actually *going.*

Jock glared at him. "I hope you're here to buy something because you're driving my customers away, so you are!"

"It's time you and I had a talk," said

Hamish. "You close at twelve-thirty, don't you? I'll be back then."

As he turned and walked out, he could feel Jock's hot and angry eyes boring into his back.

The good weather was holding and even Drim looked passably pretty in the autumn sunlight. Only the waters of the loch remained black, seeming to absorb, rather than reflect, the light from the sky above.

Hamish walked up to Peter Hynd's cottage. Mr. Apple and his builders were hard at work. He waved when he saw Hamish and walked down to the garden gate. "Everything's coming along fine," he said. "We're going to start draining the peatbog out back tomorrow."

"On the Sabbath?" Hamish looked amused. "You'll have the minister up here waving the Bible at you."

"He's already called," said Mr. Apple, leaning on the gate and taking a battered pipe and leather tobacco pouch out of his pocket. "Read me a lecture. I told him he had no right to inflict his views on me. He said that I would put up the backs of the villagers, and I pointed out that as their backs were permanently up about anything and everything, I wouldn't notice the difference. Then that wife of his turned up with some ecological mumbo-jumbo about me destroying the habitat of the rosy-breasted pushover or some damn-fool bird. All I wanted was a quiet holiday home and I think I've made a mistake coming here, but until I make up my mind what to do I'll carry on, because if I decide to sell, I mean to make sure I get my money back." Mrs. Apple, a small, sturdy woman, appeared to tell them that she had tea and scones ready and invited Hamish into their mobile home.

Hamish passed a pleasant hour with them and then walked back to the shop in time to catch Jock as he was putting up the lunch hour CLOSED sign.

"You're not here offically and you've got no right to ask me questions," growled Jock. But he turned away with Hamish and began to walk along beside the loch. "I know what you're after," said Jock, "but himself just upped and left. He was showing the signs of getting fed up with the place."

"I don't suppose *you* saw much of him," said Hamish.

"But I did, that's the odd thing. He come in for his groceries the day after the fight and he held out his hand and he said, 'I'm sorry. Women aren't worth fighting over.' And before I knew what I wass doing I had shook that hand, for at the time I thought my Ailsa had gone a bit silly about him like the other women, and you know, us men have tae stick together. After that, we chatted a bit every time he came in. He said something about he wass getting tired o' the place and might sell. I wass still a bittie jealous, so I said, 'So, you'll be kissing all the ladies goodbye,' and he said, and I think he meant it, 'I'm sick of the ladies, Jock, and that's a fact.' "

Hamish cast a quick glance at Jock's large face but could see no signs of guile or deception. He could hardly point out to Jock that his wife had been having an affair with Peter. He tried another tack.

"Look, Jock, the men must have hated him, and I believe it was you and some o' the others who heaved a brick through his window."

"You going to charge anyone?"

"Can't," said Hamish. "I'm here on holiday."

"It wass silly," said Jock. "We got that mad wi' our silly biddies flaunting themselves in front o' him. We thought we'd scare him away, and truth to tell, although he laughed about it next day, I think we did. Mind you, we got scared ourselves and left him the money for a new window on the doorstep. Don't stir things up, Hamish. This business nearly tore the village apart. Let it be."

"I could do that," said Hamish wearily, "but for the fact that Betty Baxter received a mysterious phone call, got all excited, dressed up, hair done, and went out to her death."

"Can't you chust believe she fell? That's what the police said."

"No, I can't believe that. But thanks for talking to me, Jock."

Hamish returned to Edie's, determined to take a break from his investigations and sort out his private life, but Edie told him that Priscilla had gone to Lochdubh and would be back late afternoon.

He walked off again, turning over in his mind what to say to Priscilla. Until she was prepared to let him get close, and that might never happen, it would be best to put an end to any thoughts of marriage. Also, he could change his life-style to please her but he was shrewdly sure that once they were married and the first fine careless rapture was gone, he would begin to resent her bitterly for what she had done.

He felt sad and yet could not see any alternative. He found his steps were taking him towards Jimmy Macleod's croft. Jimmy was moving sheep from one field to the other, his two collies running low, herding the beasts. Although he saw Hamish he did not raise his hand in greeting. Once the sheep were in the field, Jimmy shut the gate, whistled the dogs to heel and turned in the direction of the house. He would have walked past Hamish if Hamish had not stepped forward to block his path. "We have to talk, Jimmy," said Hamish.

"Can't you leave us alone?" muttered Jimmy.

"Look here, Jimmy, don't you want to find out what your wife has been up to?"

"No, I chust want to get on with ma' life. Leave us be."

"All right, Jimmy, I'll take the gloves off. Did it ever occur to you that there might have been something between your wife and Peter Hynd?"

Jimmy swung a blow at Hamish but Hamish caught his wrist and held it in a firm grip. "That won't solve anything. Answer me, Jimmy."

"You an' yer dirty mind," panted Jimmy. "Nancy wouldna' hae done sich a thing. She iss a good woman."

Hamish held him tightly. "She is a woman who you hit and threatened."

Jimmy began to sob, half in fury, half in a sort of despair, tears running down the wrinkles of his face.

The dogs growled softly, menacingly.

Hamish released him and stood back. "You'd feel better if you told me the truth, Jimmy. You know where I am staying. Call on me any time you feel like talking."

Jimmy scrubbed at his eyes with the rough sleeve of his jacket and then stood with his head hanging. Hamish sadly turned away. He was not like Blair and could not go on questioning anyone in such distress. He had a sudden feeling of revulsion for the whole business. Who was he, Hamish Macbeth, to go on like God Almighty? If someone had killed Peter Hynd, then good luck to them, he thought furiously. But someone who had killed and got away with it might kill again. And then what about poor, silly Betty Baxter?

He strode moodily in the direction of Edie's, his mood as black as the loch. Priscilla's car was drawn up outside Edie's. He could hear the clatter of dishes from the kitchen. No doubt efficient Priscilla was getting a nourishing lunch ready.

He stood at the entrance to the kitchen door and watched her for a minute. She was wearing tailored trousers, a white cotton blouse and a cashmere cardigan. Her blonde hair was as bright as the sunlight and she was humming under her breath, as if she didn't have a care in the world.

"Where's Edie?" he asked, moving forward. She swung round. "It's just us," she said. "Edie's gone to Strathbane with Annie Duncan to pick up the costumes, so I thought I would use the kitchen."

"Nice of you to cook lunch," said Hamish moodily, sitting down at the table.

"I'm only heating it up. It's lasagne. I got it from the restaurant in Lochdubh."

She deftly mixed a bowl of salad and then put a portion of lasagne down in front of him. He realized he was hungry and decided to put off the inevitable confrontation. He talked about Jock and Harry as he ate. "Why don't you just leave it all alone?" said Priscilla, echoing his earlier thoughts. "Look what a fool you will feel if Peter Hynd turns up alive and well. I've been thinking a lot about it. There is a danger that you yourself, Hamish, might stir the whole mess up again so much that murder will be done this time."

She put a cup of coffee in front of him.

"Maybe," he said sourly.

"I know this may be upsetting to you," she said quickly.

He pushed his cup away. "The main thing right now, Priscilla, that iss upsetting me, is us . . . you and me."

"Oh, Hamish, don't let's quarrel."

"It's past that. I thought that once we were married, you'd be more affectionate . . . warmer. But I don't think anymore that will be the case. Oh, I think I could even put up with promotion and a move to Strathbane in return for love and affection. No," he went on wearily, "I don't want a row. I'm not getting at you. It's not in you. So instead of me dragging on, hoping and hoping, I think we should drop the idea of marriage."

"I've always had trouble with . . . with that side of things," said Priscilla desperately. "Give me a little more time, just a little more time, Hamish."

"No more time." He got to his feet. "I'll go up on the Drim with my rod. Perhaps it might be a good idea if you were gone by the time I got back this evening."

He collected his rod and fishing basket from behind the door and strode off, half dreading, half hoping to hear the sound of her voice calling him back.

He fished steadily, trying to fight down a dragging, aching sense of loss, wondering how one's brain should know all the sensible answers while one's emotions longed for the unattainable. Night was falling early and frost was beginning to rime the grass when he decided to pack up. Perhaps because there was no young Heather with her pagan incantations, the fish refused to rise to the bait.

As he approached Edie's, he noticed Priscilla's car had gone. Well, it was what he had asked her to do, so why did he feel so bereft?

"Would you like a bite to eat?" asked Edie, over-bright and avoiding his eyes with a sort of awkward sympathy. "We're just on our own. Priscilla's left."

"Yes, I know," said Hamish heavily. "How did you get on in Strathbane?"

"We got the costumes all right," said Edie. "They looked awfully dusty and tacky to me, and some of them have half the sequins missing, but Annie said they would look just grand under the lights. We're trying them on this evening. Sit down and have something. It's fish pie. I made it myself."

Hamish accepted a portion of fish pie. It was quite disgusting and the pastry tasted like wet paper. He cut it up and moved it around his plate in the hope that Edie might think he had eaten some of it.

"I'll come to that rehearsal with you," said Hamish, "just to make sure there aren't any more accidents."

Edie brightened. Priscilla had said she had

to return to the hotel to work, but her face had shown signs of recent tears, and Hamish looked depressed. Correctly interpreting that the couple had had a row and that they had possibly broken up for good, Edie looked at Hamish with new eyes. He was an attractive man with his flaming red hair, hazel eyes, and shy smile. Of course he was younger than she, but still . . . And it would be gratifying to be escorted by a man to the rehearsal.

To Hamish's embarrassment, Edie took his arm as they walked towards the community hall. She smelled strongly of cheap perfume and her thin body was pressed against his side. With relief, he detached himself from her to hold the hall door open for her and then stood back to let her enter on her own.

Then he found a seat at the back of the hall. Jock Kennedy was there, arranging the lights. There were a lot of muffled giggles and scuffles from the direction of the dressing-rooms where the women were trying on their costumes. He waited, forcing his mind to concentrate on all the aspects of the case. The hall began to fill up as the women who were not in the pantomime and the men of the village came to watch. Heather was there with her father, sitting beside him, holding his hand. Most of her schoolfellows were there but Heather did not exchange one word or glance with them. Her concentration was all on her father.

The rehearsal began. Nancy, in a gown which was obviously straining at the seams, sang her song and exited without incident. Annie Duncan, as the Principal Boy, actually had a splendid pair of legs, Hamish noted. He also noticed that the minister had come in, had not taken a seat but was leaning against a pillar, his face tight with disapproval.

The choice of music was a mixture of Andrew Lloyd Webber and Scottish folk songs and a Gaelic song for the bit where everyone was supposed to join in. Heather, who had been persuaded to leave her father's side and get into her costume, made an excellent cat.

Hamish sat back with his arms folded, his eyes moving from one face to another. There was one face that was tugging at his mind. He felt it was a face he had seen before. His eyes ranged from the stage and round the audience.

By the end of the rehearsal, there was a stabbing pain over his right eye. He did not wait for Edie but went back to her house and let himself in. He sat down at the kitchen table and put his head in his hands. It was like being haunted. Something, someone he had seen at the rehearsal, was the clue to the whole affair.

Edie came in, rather huffy because he had not waited for her. She had had a lovely time at the rehearsal with Ailsa, Alice, and Nancy, hinting at a romance with Hamish, slyly implying that she, Edie, had seen Priscilla off and they had all giggled over it, quite like old times.

"Coffee?" she asked.

Hamish opened his mouth to say yes and then he looked at her blindly.

"What's the matter?" asked Edie.

"I have a headache," he said. "Got to lie down."

He went up and lay fully clothed on the bed, staring up at the ceiling. Something in his gut was telling him how it had been done and who had done it, but he had not one shred of proof, and this, he was sure, was one criminal who would not break except under extreme pressure. But how to apply that pressure?

He lay awake long into the night, falling at last into an uneasy sleep, and waking late, still in his clothes, and with all the thoughts of the night before rushing into his head. He had an urge to go to Lochdubh, to see

Priscilla, to tell her what he thought had happened and see what she said.

And then he heard a furious knocking at the door downstairs and Edie's voice raised in questioning alarm. Then he heard her running up the stairs and swung his legs out of bed and stood up, feeling dizzy and groggy.

"Come quickly, Hamish," panted Edie. "It's Mr. Apple. He's found a body."

Hamish followed the gesticulating and exclaiming builder up towards his cottage where his workmen were standing in a circle on the peatbog staring down at something.

"We were starting to drain the peatbog early," said Mr. Apple, "and to dig it up for the drains and the men found the body."

News had spread fast. People were running out of their houses.

Hamish went up to the circle of men. They parted to let him through. There, lying in the peat, was the figure of a man, black with peat mud, encrusted with peat mud. Hamish felt a red rage against the murderer, which he afterwards tried to explain allowed for his subsequent unorthodox action.

He turned to the men. "Get that body up and get it on some sort of stretcher and take it to the community hall. Get everyone in the village to the hall . . . now!"

He stood grimly while, with a terrible sucking sound, the bog gave up its prey. The blackened body was put on a door and a little procession of men carried it into the community hall. Hamish ordered them to place it on a table below the stage and stood beside it with his arms folded while the whole of the village filed in.

The minister strode to the front of the crowd. "This is disgraceful," he said. "There are children here. What do you think you are playing at?"

Hamish raised his voice. "This is the body of Peter Hynd," he said. "And the murderer of Peter Hynd is in this hall. This body may be covered in peatbog, but forensic science can do marvels these days to find out how, when, and why the man was killed. But I know who did it."

His eyes ranged over the startled faces. He sent up a prayer. He was acting on a wild hunch. But he had wanted pressure, and pressure was here in this still, dead body.

"Step forward, Annie Duncan," he said in a loud voice, "and look at what you have done."

Her face was white and drawn and she moved towards him like a sleep-walker.

"Why is he so black?" she said, her voice barely above a whisper. "I thought he would be clean with all that water. Why is he so black?"

"You did it," said Hamish. "I know you did it and I can prove it. Peter Hynd did not sign the final papers for the house sale. You did. A handwriting expert will soon prove it."

The minister found his voice. "You madman," he howled. "How dare you? Come along, Annie."

He tugged at her arm but she went on staring at Hamish as if hypnotized. "Leave me, Callum," she said quietly. "Don't you see he knows?"

"Knows what?"

"That I killed Peter Hynd."

There was an indrawn hiss of amazement from the hall. "Phone Strathbane," said Hamish to Mr. Apple, who was standing beside him. "Come with me, Mrs. Duncan."

As he led her to a side-room, he could hear a voice saying, "Thank goodness it wass not one of us. It wass an outsider." Annie Duncan had lived many years in the village but she was still regarded as an outsider.

They faced each other over a table in a side-room of the community hall. "While we're waiting for the team from Strathbane," said Hamish, "you'd better tell me how you did it and why you did it."

She gave a dry sob and then seemed to compose herself. "How did you know it was me?" she asked.

"I knew it was you when I saw you dressed as a principal boy. You had deepened your voice for the part. You are English. I realized you could have impersonated Peter. I remembered the way your face became transformed when I first called at the manse when Peter Hynd's name was mentioned. I remembered Peter's sister. She looked very like him but vaguely like you. How did you do it? Men's clothes and a blonde wig?"

She nodded.

"Why?"

She stared off into space, a blind look on her face. Then she said, "He was the most marvellous thing that had ever happened to me. He said he loved me, that we would go away together. He told me he planned to sell the house. We were above these peasants in this village, Peter and I. He was the sort of man I should have married. I had never known love like it. And then I heard the men were going to throw a brick through his window and I went to warn him, but as

I crept up to the cottage I could hear the tinkling of glass. I waited until they had gone away and I crept forward to look in the broken window. When he came down, I would call to him. He did come down. He was naked and he looked so beautiful, I stood and stared, enjoying looking at him, about to call to him. And then *she* came down from the bedroom. Silly, fat Betty Baxter, with her coarse face and her great coarse thighs. I saw them together, I saw them going up to the bedroom together, and I thought I would die of loss and shame. I think it drove me mad. Then I saw my moment. There was a film to be shown at the community hall and I knew all the village would be there. I had overheard him saying he had already seen the film in London.

"I went up to the cottage. I wanted it all to be the same. I wanted him back again. I did not think anymore of killing him. He smiled when he saw me, that blinding smile of his and I wanted to think I had imagined him with Betty. But I told him I had seen him. He looked a bit taken aback and then he began to laugh. He tugged my hair and said, 'You don't think you're the only woman in this dead-alive place that I've laid to pass the time.'

"I pleaded with him. I reminded him that

he wanted to marry me. He said, with an awful sort of indifference, 'Oh, get back to your worthy husband. It's only vanity that makes you think you're any different from the women in this village, although I suppose you are. You're more the suburban-housewife type. Now, I'm going to have a drink. You can join me or you can go.' He went into the other room, I suppose to get the bottle of whisky. I saw a hammer lying on the floor of the extension. I went and picked it up and hefted it in my hand. He came back and went over to the counter and took down a glass. My hand seemed to take on a life of its own. I struck him as hard as I could. He fell to the floor, stone dead. And I was glad. I worked like the devil. He had only a few sticks of furniture, so I knew nobody would think it odd that he might include them in the house sale. I took everything else and loaded it up in his car except the papers and title deeds and bank-books and cards, which I took back to the manse later. I backed the car up to the door, his car, and put his body in the boot. I loaded up his car, like I said. I got into the driving seat and free-wheeled slowly down past the community hall. I had the car windows open and could see the lights in the hall and hear the sound of laughter.

When I was down past the hall, I started the engine and drove to the end of the loch, to the deep part, to that ledge which hangs over it. I switched off the engine. I got out and I pushed the car over and watched it sink down like a stone into the black water.

"I went back to his cottage and scrubbed the blood from the floor and scrubbed every surface I could see. I had kept his typewriter back, along with the papers. I took it home with me, typed the letter to Jock, and put it with the key through the letter-box at the shop. The next day I couldn't believe I had done it."

Hamish looked at her in bewilderment. "But the body was found in the peatbog."

"The what?"

"Thon body was found in the peatbog at the back of Apple's cottage. Didn't you know?"

She shook her head. "Someone came running up to tell us we were to come to the community hall. That was all." She stared at him and then began to laugh harshly. "Wrong body," she said. Hamish rose and went outside and told one of the waiting men to phone Strathbane and order a team of frogmen. Then he returned to Annie, determined to worry about the strange peatbog body when he had got her full confession.

"And Betty Baxter?" he said when he had sat down again.

She sighed heavily. "Betty had become over-familiar with me. I like the women to know their place and keep their distance, and it was borne in on me that Peter had told her about his affair with me, had probably laughed over it with her and God knows who else. I hated her. I thought I would play a trick on her. I phoned her and said I was Peter and asked her to meet me on the beach the following morning and then sat back and enjoyed the spectacle of Betty wild with excitement, getting her hair done, running about in a glow of triumph.

"I saw her standing by the rocks, her gross body supported on those ridiculous heels, and I thought, Oh, Peter, *how could you?* I had meant to jeer at her, to see the look of disappointment on her face. But I gave her a great push in her great fat back. Why didn't she put her hands out to save herself? I couldn't believe it when I found she was dead. I ran away."

"How could you live with yourself?" marvelled Hamish.

"Betty's death was an accident, not murder. I put it out of my mind. I was waiting until things all died down and then I planned to leave Callum and go back to London. But you had to turn up with your gawky amateur probing." She began to laugh again. "And you got the wrong body."

She was still laughing and weeping when the team from Strathbane arrived.

CHAPTER 11

When we were a soft amoeba, in ages
    past and gone,
Ere you were the Queen of Sheba, or I
    King Solomon,
Alone and undivided, we lived a life of
    sloth,
Whatever you did, I did; one dinner served
    for both.
Anon came separation, by fission and di-
    vorce,
A lonely pseudopodium I wandered on my
    course.

                Sir Arthur Shipley

"So," said detective Jimmy Anderson gleefully, "you've been reduced to the ranks,
Hamish. Stripped o' yer stripes, and nae
wonder. You dig up a fine example o' Pict-
ish man in a bog, accuse a minister's wife o'
murdering it, and she confesses to mur-

dering Peter Hynd. Och, we havena' had such a laugh down at Strathbane for years and years."

Anderson and Hamish were sitting in the police office at Lochdubh several days later, sharing a bottle of whisky.

"Man, man," said Anderson, pouring another shot of Scotch, "I think the super must have had complaints from every prof, museum, and archaeological society from here to Australia. Such a valuable relic in the hands of a clod-hopping policeman."

"Oh, shut up," said Hamish moodily. "Do you know what got to all of you lazy fools in Strathbane? It wass that I knew there had been the murder, and proved it too."

"Aye, you did that. Car in the loch, body in the boot, and Hynd's typewriter up at the manse. What put you on to her?"

"It was when I saw her on the stage dressed up as a principal boy with her hair pushed up under one of those Tudor hats. I remembered thinking that she made a fine-looking man. I had been uneasy about her in the back of my mind, or I must have been. It wass her vanity, you see. Priscilla told me she seemed to think herself a good cut above the women of the village, and I could see that vanity in the way she strutted about the stage and the way she ordered the women about during that rehearsal. But she had seemed such a controlled and quiet woman that her vanity was not immediately evident. She was the only one in the village with the sophistication to keep cool and to plan, and to impersonate Peter. I don't know how I knew it, but I somehow knew Peter had been killed and one o' them had done it. I'm right glad it didn't turn out to be Harry Baxter."

"It's a wonder it wasn't that cold wee daughter o' his."

"Och, the lassie wasnae cold at all," said Hamish. "She wass chust holding herself together because she loves her father and she thought he had done it. When she heard about Annie, she broke down and cried her eyes out wi' relief that the nightmare wass over for her. It was her that put me on to it. She came here one night and said she had seen the murder of Peter in her head."

"Well, it's all over," said Anderson, "although I could do without Blair being so happy about your demotion. Then the super got to hear from his wife that your engagement was at an end and that made you even more of a failure, Hamish. Aye, and there's something else."

"There can't be," said Hamish, reaching for the bottle.

"But there is. Do you ken a wee man called Hendry, school-teacher?"

"The wife-beater? What's happened?"

"He's put in a complaint about you."

"What did he say, not but what it'll be all lies," added Hamish quickly, thinking of how he had banged the school-teacher's head into the wall.

"He says you got his missus into some sort o' brainwashing cult."

"Havers. I suggested she go to Al-Anon."

"Aye, well, so she did, and she put the children into Ala-Teen. That house, Craig-allen, was in her name. She's got her ain money. Well, she sells the house, pockets the money, takes the kids and goes off tae Glasgow saying she's finished wi' being a martyr, and the wee drunk man she married can either come tae his senses or drink himself tae death. It looks as if he's chosen the latter solution."

"But surely Strathbane didn't take the complaint seriously?"

"Relax, they didn't. Blair was all for sobering Hendry up and presenting him to the super, but Hendry had a half bottle in his pocket and showed no signs of wanting to sober up. So what are you going to do with yourself now?"

"Same as I did before," said Hamish.

"Police Lochdubh and stay as far away from Strathbane as possible. Is Annie Duncan still talking?"

"Aye, and the more she talks, the weirder she gets. Now she's over the shock o' being caught, she seems almost proud of what she's done."

"It's odd," said Hamish. "When the estate agents reported that Peter Hynd had had a bad cold and was muffled up to the eyebrows, I thought that must be someone impersonating him. But that was him. It was her that signed the final papers. It's come out that he did have a bad cold. And now they tell me happily about the night of the film show. If they had told me before and I had learned that Peter wasn't there, then I would have known that was the ideal time to get rid of him. Did the minister know about his wife's affair while it was going on?"

"Annie says he didn't know a thing," said Jimmy. "In fact, she says the one great thing about going to prison is that she'll get away from him. Makes ye think hanging a good idea."

Anderson drained the last Scotch from the bottle into his glass, tossed it off and got to his feet. "I'd better be off, Hamish. Can't be caught socializing wi' the enemy.

See you around at the next murder."

Hamish sat with his feet up on the desk after Anderson had left. He had a sudden impulse to go to Drim and see how they were all settling down. He could not drive because he had drunk well over the limit, and so he got up and went out to the shed at the back and wheeled out a rusty bike and set off up the hill on it.

It was a steel-grey day and the air was heavy with the metallic smell of approaching snow. He almost wished he had not decided on this trip as he weaved his way down the winding road which led into Drim and saw the black waters of the loch and the stark bleakness of the surrounding mountains. He went straight to Harry Baxter's. It was a Sunday, and so he knew the fisherman would be at home. Harry was watching television.

"Where's Heather?" asked Hamish.

"She's out playing wi' her friends."

"That's grand," said Hamish.

"Aye, she doesnae need to worry about me anymore. Can you imagine," said Harry in awe, "that she thocht I'd done it?"

"Well, it's over now. No more rows, I hope?"

Harry grinned. "I don't know about that. We're getting the new minister and he's a young man and no' married, so Alice's shop is busy again and Edie's started the exercise classes."

"Oh, dear. What about the pantomime?"

"They stopped that and sent the costumes back. I thocht Heather would be disappointed not to play the cat but she didnae seem to mind."

Hamish dug into his pockets and took out a handful of paperbacks. "I brought some books for Heather. Though she won't be needing them so much now." He put them on the table.

"Thanks," said Harry, his eyes straying back to the television set, where one furry puppet was savagely hitting another.

Hamish went down towards the community hall. The old familiar sound of music reached his ears. He had a pang of dread that rivalry over this minister would start the old feuds. He looked towards the manse and saw there was a furniture-delivery van outside.

He cycled up. He called to one of the workmen, "Is the minister in?"

The man jerked his head towards the kitchen door.

Hamish walked in. The new minister turned to meet him. He was a small fat man with thinning hair. He had very thick pebble glasses. He looked like a toad.

Hamish stepped forward with a smile of pure relief and gladness on his face and wrung the minister's hand. "Welcome to Drim," he said.

When he returned to Lochdubh, he saw Phil Jameson, a young man who did odd jobs about the village, and called to him. "Got a job for you, Phil."

"Whit's that?" asked Phil, padding over and wiping his hands on his overalls.

"Come with me," said Hamish. He led Phil to the shed at the back and pointed to the wood-burning stove. "I want that put back in the kitchen and the new electric taken out."

"Can do," said Phil laconically. "Selling the electric?"

"No, put that on your truck and take it to Tommel Castle Hotel and give it to Miss Halburton-Smythe with my compliments."

"That's finished, I hear," said Phil.

"Aye, well, mind your own business. I'm off to Rogart to get my dog."

The phone from the police station rang shrilly. He went in to answer it. It was Edie Aubrey. "Hamish," she said, "I've found out who tripped Nancy on the stairs."

"Who was it?"

"It was Ailsa. She told Nancy and asked her to forgive her."

"And does Nancy forgive her?"

"Oh, yes, they're as thick as thieves, but I don't see why Ailsa should get away with it. You should —"

"Edie," interrupted Hamish, "have you seen the new minister?"

"Not yet."

"He's at the manse. Go and have a look and then ask yourself whether you want Ailsa charged with anything."

And one look at that ugly minister, thought Hamish, as he put the phone down, will be enough to cool their fevered dreams. They were probably expecting another Adonis.

The next phone call was from his cousin Rory in London, very angry because Hamish had not given him an advance story on the murder. "If you'd got me up there," said Rory, "I could have stopped you making such a fool of yourself by accusing someone of murdering a man out of a peat-bog who'd been dead for centuries."

"Leave it be," said Hamish. "I found the murderer and the real body. I've had enough criticism and been demoted, and I don't want any more complaints."

But there was more to come. For when he

went to his parents in Rogart, he had to listen to his mother's gentle complaints about "losing" Priscilla.

He was in a filthy mood by the time he returned to the police station. Snow was beginning to fall heavily. In the kitchen, the wood-burning stove once more stood in the corner. He felt petty and mean at having sent back the stove to Priscilla. He wanted to phone her and apologize but could not bear the thought of hearing her voice.

He piled up the stove with logs. The stove drew even better than it had ever done before. He fed Towser and made dinner for himself.

What had he left in life? he thought. Demoted back to constable, no more Priscilla, back to his old life. The wind howled outside and snow whispered against the window-panes. The stove roared and glowed red, steak sizzled in the pan, and suddenly the police station seemed a refuge against a naughty world outside.

"Yes, I'm back to where I was," said Hamish to Towser.

He turned the steak in the pan and began to whistle.

We hope you have enjoyed this Large Print book. Other Thorndike, Wheeler, and Chivers Press Large Print books are available at your library or directly from the publishers.

For information about current and upcoming titles, please call or write, without obligation, to:

Publisher
Thorndike Press
295 Kennedy Memorial Drive
Waterville, ME 04901
Tel. (800) 223-1244

or visit our Web site at:

www.gale.com/thorndike
www.gale.com/wheeler

OR

Chivers Large Print
published by BBC Audiobooks Ltd
St James House, The Square
Lower Bristol Road
Bath BA2 3SB
England
Tel. +44(0) 800 136919
email: bbcaudio books@bbc.co.uk
www.bbcaudiobooks.co.uk

All our Large Print titles are designed for easy reading, and all our books are made to last.